WAKI

# WAKE UP

## TIM PEARS

BLOOMSBURY

First published in Great Britain 2002
This paperback edition published 2003

Copyright © Tim Pears 2002

Grateful acknowledgement is made to Syngenta Crop Protection UK Ltd,
Whittlesford, Cambridge to reprint excerpts from promotional material for
Zeneca Crop Protection titled 'Guide to Potato Diseases and their Control'.

The moral right of the author has been asserted

Bloomsbury Publishing Plc, 38 Soho Square, London W1D 3HB

A CIP catalogue record is available from the British Library

ISBN 0 7475 6153 2
10 9 8 7 6 5 4 3 2 1

Typeset by Palimpsest Book Production Limited,
Polmont, Stirlingshire
Printed by Clays Ltd, St Ives plc

## DEDICATION

To my father Bill, *in memoriam*,
and my son Gabriel,
whose genes gave birth to this book.

# ACKNOWLEDGEMENTS

The author is profoundly grateful to The Lannan Foundation for providing a retreat in New Mexico, land of old spirits and new messages, as the twentieth century passed into the twenty-first.

Even more than usual special thank you to Alexandra Pringle, indispensable editor. Thanks also to Hania Porucznik, Victoria Hobbs and Pawel Pawlikowski for vital feedback.

The author is greatly indebted to Alan Owens, Chief Executive of Greenvale AP plc, and Steve Gerrish at the British Potato Council, for generously giving of their time and minds. Also to Valleri Longcoy and Dwayne D. Kirk of the Edible Vaccines Project at Boyce Thompson Institute for Plant Research at Cornell University, Ithaca, New York, for sharing and elucidating research material. None of these persons are responsible for how the author has fictionalised the information they gave.

Amongst sources consulted, special mention should be made of: *The Potato*, Larry Zuckerman, Macmillan, 1999. *The History and Social Influence of the Potato*, Redcliffe Salaman, Cambridge University Press, 1949/1989. *The Story of the Potato*, Alan Wilson, Henry Doubleday Research Association, 1993. *Darkness in El Dorado*, Patrick Tierney, W.W. Norton & Co, 2000. *potatoes – from gnocchi to mash*, Annie Nichols, Ryland Peters & Small, 1998. *Students for Sale*, Steven Manning and Ray Langley, Crosswinds and The Nation, December 16–23, 1999.

# MONDAY 7.45 A.M.

HOW AM I going to tell Greg?
I'll tell him when I get to work. I'm driving, around the ring road. I don't *have* to go to work, today or any other damned day; we own the company. What's the point of owning your own business if not so a man can stay at home when he doesn't feel like going to work?

Someone died.

I love going to work. Owning the company's a veto. I've never invoked it. And neither, for that matter, has Greg.

But isn't a man allowed once in a while to do things a little differently?

It's not that I want to stay at home. It's not that. No, I think I'd rather just keep driving around the ring road. Ease back, relax. Let the present drift.

I remember we were driving, Lily and I. A year ago, just the two of us. In a hire car, night was approaching, we'd booked a room in a remote hotel for a long weekend and were headed there.

A man leaves the obligation, the ambition, of existence behind even for a weekend and the weight falls away. A filling station passed us by, but there was plenty of fuel in the tank. We'd nattered on the plane, Heathrow–Rome, and now were silent. Lily put her hand on my thigh. I drove.

The landscape widened: no more villages, sporadic dwellings. We began to run low on petrol, the roads became quieter, and at a certain point I realised that the garage we'd passed was quite probably the last one. The fuel-gauge needle drooped through the final quarter of the tank.

Darkness gathered. I was lying just now, by the way. It was Birmingham–Glasgow. It was Scotland. There's nothing wrong with Scotland. I'm no cheapskate. It wasn't some cheap weekend deal. Actually, it was, now I think about it; Lily spotted it in a Sunday travel section.

Dusk fell. Entering forestry land, the needle dipped into the reserve. I estimated that we were some forty miles short of our isolated hotel, where they'd either have their own supply of petrol or be able to obtain some. A red light came on, indicating, I assumed, some twenty-five miles' worth of gas. Trees shouldered the road in the dark. Lights from remote homes dwindled to none.

Fraught up in my anxiety and annoyance, Lily's voice startled me. 'We should have filled up at that last petrol station,' she said.

I ignored her. Anger ran silent as rain through my veins. What did I do? I put my foot down, didn't I? I drove faster. I knew how stupid it was, that I should have eased off the accelerator, cruised at forty, the better to conserve whatever meagre fuel remained in the tank. Instead I raced towards our destination, thus to reach it before the fuel ran out. I couldn't help myself.

'You do this, John,' Lily said. 'This is one of your quirks, isn't it? Seeing how empty you can let the tank get before filling up. Seeing how much petrol you can fit in in one go.'

I was concentrating on the road ahead, but even when you can't see them, you can tell when someone's shaking their head.

2

Lily was shaking hers. 'Even in a hire car. If you can put off stopping to fill up until you've got the needle below empty, you score a small victory. Over whom? How, exactly? Why? Sweetheart,' she said, 'it's an obsessive compulsive disorder. You should get it seen to.'

She was right. I *do* do that, and I'd just done it again, and I do other mental things too. Like, I get snagged on certain numbers. On threes of particular objects. Driving, I go through phases of counting off what I see in threes. One, two, three bungalows. For a few minutes at a time. One, two, three women drivers. One, two, three telegraph poles. Everybody does this kind of thing, though, don't they?

Lily said, 'And then something like this happens. I mean, wake up, sweetheart. I know this is going to be a walking weekend, but I hadn't planned on starting tonight.'

But the thing is not the petrol, no, it's not the failure to fill up with petrol. It's putting my foot down on the accelerator. Lily hadn't noticed that I was doing this, or perhaps she had but didn't twig what an obtuse response to the predicament it was. There we were, driving into pitch-black wilderness, running on empty through the looming pines, and I was using up gas as fast as I could.

This behaviour was untypical, by the way. I ought to make that clear. Unlike me. Like my brother, yes, sure; the kind of kneejerk you expect from Greg. But I'm not like that. I'm cool and rational. That's me, anyone would agree.

Yet there we were, hurtling towards an infuriating crisis.

And that is what they're doing, isn't it? It's what human beings have been doing ever since they came out of the forest, they're just doing it faster than ever. Speeding. We've scampered across the surface of this planet, and gone tripping into space. Now we're exploring the infinity within. What are we doing? Are we out of control? I wish I knew. Where are we going? No one knows. All I know is, someone's got to get there first.

What are we doing? I suppose we're growing. We're growing into ourselves. Am I right? Maybe I'm wrong.

Oh, people don't understand.

I'll turn off the ring road next time round. For the moment I'm easing along at fifty-five miles per hour. Hey, what's this guy doing up my behind? Lorries, they come looming up on top of you and leave it till the last second. Then swing out on some invisible pivot. Go on. Go past, friend.

I'm cruising. Lorry driver, what a job. Why would anyone do that? Why? Because he's got responsibilities, that's why. He's got a family to support. And that woman in the Metro, there: is she a mother? People have kids.

I've got one. People thought I couldn't, didn't they? Well, I have now. How about that? How strange and beautiful a thing.

# Gangrene

Irregular, dark, sunken areas on tubers.
Skin initially stretched tight, becoming wrinkled.
Internally large cavities; distinct boundary between
damaged and healthy tissue.
Bacterial wet rots can follow.

## MONDAY 8.15 A.M.

W E'RE STOP-STARTING around the ring road. I'm normally out of the village by seven-fifteen and beat the rush hour. How odd it must be to do this every day, to play these shadow dodgems. To lurch and brake and stall, create motional syncopations. An improvising, automotive orchestra.

But what am I doing? I really ought to get to work. I need to talk with Greg. Tell him the news. Tell him everything. And I will. I'm not scared of my brother. What am I, some quaking youth? Hardly. An anxious old man? Hold on. No, it's just rather fun, jerking to and fro in the ring-road rush hour.

Two people have died, out of twenty-four who took part in the trial. I don't see how it's possible to prove they died because they took part. We accept that smoking can cause lung cancer. My father smoked forty a day: Dad died of cancer, but it's possible he would have even if he'd never smoked a single cig. Wasn't it his stomach, too? So they can't be sure. No, I think Simon's overreacting.

I'm forty-five years old. As those excitable optimists we fund at AlphaGen assured me on my last birthday, I'm in the middle of my life. Indeed, they ventured, such was the accelerating pace of certain colleagues' research out digging in the gene fields, there's real hope that I may remain in this hypothetical median for years to come. Whatever, and allowing for their geeky humour, I am surely in my prime.

I said this same thing to Lily. 'His prime,' my gentle wife hiccuped. 'In the life of your libido?' she demanded. 'Oh, of your professional life, you mean?' Then, turning to an imaginary figure who took up residence in our marriage a year or two ago and seems to lurk in a corner of our bedroom, Lily said, 'We're dreaming of another million, and we're in our prime already.' She turned back to me. 'Sweetheart,' she said. 'Wake up, why don't you?'

Nineteen weeks ago a child was born to us. In the morning Lily sleeps in alone while in the spare room Jacob dozes beside me. Then he is peaceful, but much of his life he spends besieged, by storms that brew up within him. Like last night's torrid bout of teething: he woke and cried, but with his eyes tight shut, neither fully awake nor asleep. Tears escaping from his scrunched-up eyes. Wailing. I have to jolt him out of this state, and the best way seems to be to whisk him to the bathroom, there to hold him in front of that mirror with lights around it. The light opens his eyes, and he is surprised by the sight of himself, and then of me, holding him. And he may forget the pain his teeth are causing him, at least for long enough for camomilla, or in a dire case baby paracetamol, to take effect.

Our son's tempestuous, untamed body. After feeding, he possets a runny goo over his – and his mother's – clothes. Then he hiccups. He pees, and poos. Sometimes he jumps with an electrical start, tossed on the flux, the nervous whirlpool, that is his body.

Greg and I were a partnership from the beginning, from the day I joined him on two legs. A person might not have thought so back then. As a baby, Dad maintained, Greg used to beat up our mother. Pulled her hair, poked her in the eye. Even as a tiny sprog, he headbutted her, squeezed her sore nipples, kicked her in the stomach. Mum was never free of bruises. Yet he couldn't bear to be apart, to be separated from her, for a second; Greg clung to his mother like an angry chimp. She couldn't put him down even to perform her ablutions: had to undress him and herself together and share every bath she took; had to use the toilet with him on her lap. Imagine that.

And neither would nor could Greg sleep unless attached to her, preferably spreadeagled across her chest, while Mum lay back at a forty-five degree angle. Greg spread his arms wide beneath her breasts, red cheek pressed to her breastbone, his tummy resting on hers, his short, stout legs tapering down to twitching feet. Ankles tensing and untensing. His toes plied her pubic hair, dug around her muff.

Is there one word to describe my brother as a baby? Frantic. The extraordinary thing is that he managed to project the aura of a victim, of someone wronged. Greg lay open-mouthed across our mother's generous body as if crucified.

'You been beating up Mum again?' Dad would say when he spotted another bruise. My brother gazed back at Dad over Mum's shoulder with placid disdain.

The first recognisable emotion Greg expressed was that of jealousy. Of our father; and then of me when I appeared. He clung on to Mum all the more, forced her to wean this unwanted rival in weeks. When our sister was born, a further two years on, my brother's sense of grievance intensified. People might agree it was my turn for a streak of sibling spleen, but no: Greg grabbed all the rage that was going. He was furious. For months his tantrums were storms you just toddled out of the way of. I remember them well.

9

The curious fact is, though, that I felt no envy of Greg's place so tenaciously held. Really. I accepted my older brother as he was.

Greg was infuriated by Melody's arrival, but eventually he came to his senses and joined the rest of us in our disbelieving, protective attitude towards her.

'My one-shot wonder,' our father used to call Melody. I had no idea what he meant back then. 'Our one-shot wonder girl.' He'd look at Greg and say, 'I still don't know how I prised you and your mum apart for long enough for one one-shot wonder.'

We grew up, my brother and I, and our undeserving sister too, in the stink of rotting fruit and vegetables. And I'll never forget this: that once they begin to rot, fruit and veg may smell very different. One sickeningly sweet, the other putrid. But you can't tell, because when they rot together the whole mess smells the same. Mildewed oranges, limp lettuce, soggy plums, they aspire towards the same putrefaction. Lily says that with minimal intervention our father could have had a crumbly, odourless, compost, but she can't imagine what it was like. Decomposing tomatoes, rank cabbage, all around you all the time.

Did we have to endure this? Yes. Why? Because our father was chaotic and overworked, gone from the house before dawn, returning at odd moments through the day, lurching into the yard with a beep of the van's horn that ordered anyone who was around to run out and help load up. But mainly because it was his policy to keep the produce a day too long. It's a critical question when dealing with perishable goods: do you throw stuff away as soon as it's lost its bloom, chuck your capital on the dung heap, in the hope of attracting more customers drawn to the pristine quality of what you sell? Our father couldn't bring himself to do that, poor bastard. He took the other option: to drop prices. Week-old carrots only so much, soft pears half-price. It was a perfectly valid approach: he had mean customers who came to his stall expressly to buy the cheapest veg on the market; one elderly hunchback I remember, and the stale stink of his tobacco-smoked coat, who relied on our father to cater for his taste in overripe bananas.

But certainly our dad's approach contributed to the chaos in the yard at home around the trailer. Crates of browning, mouldy veg brought back still unsold were simply dragged out of the van and abandoned – in contrast to the care with which he built unstable pyramids of fruit on the stall and arranged colours like a florist.

Our father never emptied or hosed down the earthen yard; he just moved what was near to our nominally mobile but actually stationary home further away, to some half-vacant spot in a corner where it could rot into the ground. No clearout, only this turgid movement around the compound.

Dad didn't get it. Growth is necessary. Growth is not some contrived sub-clause in the laws of capitalism. It's the primal force that capitalism springs from, reflects, is sustained by.

Greg and I shared a room, and he always woke up a few minutes after me, and in the same way: less like someone who'd fallen asleep the previous evening than one who'd been punched into unconsciousness. A radio-alarm clock Greg had saved up weeks of pocket money for flipped pop music in the air. My brother looked groggily around, blinked a few times, then closed his eyes and jiggled his head like a dog to shake loose the last drops of his dreams. Sometimes he ran his open palm down over his face. Until, having ascertained whose body he inhabited and where it was he happened to find himself on this earth, that morning, Greg swept aside the covers and sprang into action without a backward glance, making for the bathroom or kitchen at a trot.

We can almost see the old place in a minute. There was no ring road then. It's coming up – there, somewhere between the two high rises. I can't say where exactly. All built over now. They were building all through our childhood, one of the largest municipal projects in the country; our plot a final gap filled in. A council house or two must sit on squidgy foundations. I wonder whether the smell still rises?

Greg and I – and Melody when she joined us – played with Dad's empty crates and pallets and boxes. Construction. We built our own dolls' houses. We saw how it was done, after all, this vast council estate going up around us and a few other trailer families. Greg was the builder, I was more the architect. We devised streets, blocks, we put whole shanty towns together, Greg's remote-control racing car crashing around corners.

In summer, the smell was truly terrible. Even we could tell that, habituated to it as we were. People would stop to yell, 'There's something wrong with your drains.' It was the stink of rotting vegetables.

Mum was inside, harassing fresh ones. For our mother and most of her generation, cooking meant subjecting food to varied forms of assault that drained it of taste. Roast potatoes soggy with cooking oil. Baked potatoes, leathery hand grenades. Boiled potatoes falling apart on the plate.

Our mobile home hadn't moved an inch on its platform of breeze blocks since the day it was delivered, direct from the factory, and positioned atop a concrete base. As if the word 'mobile' denoted neither unwanted transience nor dream of upwards, downwards, sideways mobility, but boasted only of its beginnings: our home's materialisation in an empty spot, on a vacant stage.

Not that I myself saw this act of sorcery: it occurred shortly before I was born, when Greg was a year old. But it's not hard to imagine, since I saw the magic repeated on a couple of nearby plots, before the houses began to go up. These occasions have coalesced to form a single early memory. Men shuttering off a plot with planks of wood; covering the ground with old bricks, stones, broken china; filling a concrete mixer with shovelfuls of sand, cement, pebbles and water; pouring the resultant grey gloop on to the ground.

A man, kneeling on a plank, tamped down the wet concrete with a wide strip of wood that jutted out over each side of shuttering. He shuffled forward, scraping the excess off the top and away from himself. The pebbles disappeared into the grey swamp.

I can picture Dad performing this task, even though I know I couldn't have seen him doing ours. Maybe he helped one of our neighbours. Whether this is a fake memory or a real one, I see Dad working twice as fast as any other layer of concrete ever did, because that's how he was. Tilting wheelbarrows of broken bricks with a dusty roar. Hurling shovelfuls of sand into the mixer like a torpedo loader in a black and white wartime sub. Tamping down the concrete so fast the seesaw tap of wood on wood hammers out a staccato percussion.

To each expectant plot would come, early one subsequent morning, a leviathan of the roads: a huge low-loader, flashing lights and festooned with red flags like bunting, bearing the WIDE LOAD of a mobile home. A crowd gathered: the event was carnivalesque. Like the appearance of a battleship in the harbour of our neighbourhood, the vehicle drew to a slow rest with self-important grunts and sighs and groans, and from it a new home was lifted on to breeze blocks dragged and shuffled into position by half a dozen scuttling men.

We were a blue-eyed, plug-ugly Anglo-Saxon family. Yes, we were. White and skinny or white and lumpy: that was the choice our genes offered us. My father had a childish kind of face, without depth; small eyes, nose, mouth popped on a spherical head. He was balding, yet instead of ageing him this merely exacerbated the infantile roundness of his cranium. He was like a cartoon character whose creator refused to allow him to age, to mature, to learn more. Our mother had a fine-boned, delicate, feeble face, that of an anxious bird, but her body was short and bulging, low bosom and tubular waist persuading clothes out of their manufactured shape and into hers. My brother too was stocky and his features were squashed and pugnacious, while myself, I was stringy like Dad and plain, neither noticed nor remembered. A friend once told me I had a Photofit face.

'Steer clear of crime, John,' he advised me.

And out of the midst of this bunch, this unpromising thicket of genes, rose a pretty, slender girl who appeared to share not a single trait with any one of us. Almond-eyed, brown-skinned, poised. Melody. She made my blood hum.

Four of our family formed a proud praetorian guard around the fifth, this adopted young princess. I understood that was what we looked like. My parents, my brother and I guarding a young member of foreign royalty, temporarily fostered with as humdrum an English household as possible. Melody gave our family a fairy tale dimension.

My brother liked to frighten Mum. He used to imitate birds. No, not birds, it wasn't birds, it was flying pterodactyls, made of Plasticine and filmed in stuttering animation gobbling up semi-clothed actors. They cawed like hoarse

14

ravens when they, i.e. he, crouched on sideboards and windowsills and swooped down on Mum's shoulders as she passed by.

Do all small boys zigzag through a period of insanity around the age of six or seven? When they make funny sounds explicable only to themselves, jump up in the air, dash in and out of rooms for no apparent reason?

Greg regularly brought home from primary school a thick ear or black eye that he explained reluctantly. 'I had to sort X out,' he would say sadly. 'Y was asking for it,' he'd sigh. After the jealousy of his first years Greg never fought with me or any other member of the family. It could have been that he'd flushed such antagonistic behaviour from his system, but I think it more likely that a mental shift took place: you faced out from your circle, and fought the world. It became unconscionable for Greg to turn his violence inward upon those close to him, it would have meant turning his moral radar inside out.

He was a wonderful older brother. Because of Greg, no one bothered me. 'Call me on this walkie-talkie if you're in trouble, John.' He afforded me space to work out for myself who I wanted as friends, allies, enemies. To make my own calculations. No one wanted to mix it with Greg. He wasn't tall, by the time I was ten or eleven I'd caught him up. But Greg was not merely bullish, he was unstoppable. Other boys could overcome him, but they could never subdue him. If they put Greg on the floor, he'd get up again. If they hurt him badly he'd nurse wound and grudge together: he'd recuperate and come back for more. No one wants to fight that kind of relentless aggravation, the kind they'll never be rid of.

My first calculation was that I should keep close to my older brother. Or perhaps I should say, keep him close to me.

*       *       *

15

From the moment the world came into her focus, a smile was rarely absent from Melody's countenance. The baby we coddled, the toddler we jostled each other to spoil, Mum admonishing, 'She'll get ideas above her station,' this baby smiled indulgently up at a crescent of fools' faces. These games, these songs, these peek-a-boos, Melody responded to more like a benevolent judge of some talent contest than the audience of one for whom the show was put on. She was a self-composed child.

It was the same with her friends. Other girls schemed for intimacy with the prettiest girl in school. They prowled the playground in shifting packs, allegiances sworn in blood and broken in spite, tears spilt over snide, precise cruelties. I caught glimpses of such female strategy even in Melody's class, two years below me and across the gender divide, of which Melody herself appeared quite unaware.

The friends she brought home were unpredictable. There might be one of the other glamorous figures in her class, but they could just as well be misfits and oddballs. Like Jimmy Green, a boy who had to stare at people or objects or his own thoughts before responding to them. As if he had to peer into the essence of a thing, had to have a long hard look at you before knowing how to address you. Melody let Jimmy hang around our place for a few months, spooking Mum in the kitchen whenever she turned round to find this wide-eyed silent kid staring at her.

Or there was Sally something, her surname's gone, who liked to pretend that she was disabled in some way. That she lacked one of her senses. I once came across Melody and Sally in the warehouse, as Dad called his wooden storage shed, with their eyes closed, opening boxes and identifying contents by shape, texture, smell. Describing them.

'It's smoother than a peach,' said Melody. 'It's not as waxy as an apple. It's a pear. But it's not shaped like a pear.'

'So what variety is it?' Sally demanded.

'I don't know,' Melody admitted, eyes screwed tight shut as if by an exaggerated frown of ignorance. 'I forget that stuff.'

The last to open their eyes was the winner of this game, and Sally and Melody were able to play it for hours, being equally honest and incurious people. I tried to join them but couldn't restrain myself from peeking. Another time they built a wobbly tower of fruit and a vegetable dome with their eyes placidly closed. I grew instantly impatient watching them, although funnily enough they inspired a habit I retain today: when checking a batch of potatoes I close my eyes and concentrate on the way they feel, and smell.

I'm reminded of one occasion. I wasn't much of a disobedient child, but one lunchtime I got it into my head to throw my food on the floor. No toddler, mind, I was six or seven years old. I have no excuse, I knew what I was doing. The idea surged into my head to throw food on the floor and I did so, methodically, a spoonful at a time.

'John!' Mum said. 'What do you think you're ...? Stop that.'

I continued.

'Pick that up, John. Stop it at once.'

Greg and Melody just stared, as if waiting for some sense in what I was doing to reveal itself.

I remember looking up at Mum with what I knew to be insolence and defiance. She crumbled, whisked away my plate and began clearing the mess off the floor herself, saying, 'Wait till your father gets home, young man. We'll see what Dad thinks of this.'

Sure, Dad came home, took me to their bedroom, gave me a good belt across my bare backside. We danced that duet a few times. But it's Mum I'm thinking of. What was I doing? I don't know, asserting myself, of course, that's easy to say. But it looks to me now rather as if I was bullying her.

Greg was and is Mum's favourite, it was an open secret. Melody was too perfect and different from her to give Mum that wrench of love in her stomach. Greg spent his infancy beating Mum up and she adores him. Adored Dad too in her way. I remember she used to say of our father, 'He's the sort of man who sweeps leaves in the wind.' Not said aggressively, no, she was timidly teasing him. With pride, indeed. Accompanied by a shake of the head, and a frail laugh. 'My husband, he's the sort of man who sweeps leaves in the wind.' As if to say, Yes, he's stubborn, my old man, he doesn't give a monkey's what people think of him; he's eccentric, he's an individualist. He's individually mine.

Though she was right in another sense: our father only thought of sweeping leaves, it only occurred to him to do so, when presented with the sight of them being blown around our yard. And then he couldn't wait. He'd go and grab a rake or a broom and condemn himself to a mighty Canute-like encounter. He was unable to put off such a task to a more suitable time. Dad lived in an always now or never.

Our father had a way of adding certain words to the end of sentences that implied that what he'd just said contained depth one might have missed on first hearing. 'Council's taxing traders off the street. Carry on like this there won't be any markets,' he'd say, and then: 'You see what I'm saying?'

Or, 'Your grandmother was born while Queen Victoria

was still alive. She's seen two centuries. Haven't you, Nan? Think about it, boy. See what I'm driving at?'

By the age of nine or ten I already wanted to yell at my father, 'Of course we can see what you're driving at, Dad! It's a straight bloody line!'

His customers were more indulgent than me, his son. Or no more intelligent than him, perhaps. It's a confusing moment when a boy begins to apprehend that he's brighter than his father. Not to mention an irritation. Nor an embarrassment.

I mustn't draw an inaccurate picture. Our father was excitable, tense, too busy for solemnity. He was a work-aholic, a bony, blurred figure lifting sacks of spuds and boxes of apples and crates of caulis in and out of the van. *Sharpe's Fresh Produce.* Juddering out of the yard with a fart of putrid exhaust smoke. Dad was like a child, that's what it was, he jumped with excitement. He often got hiccups. He drank milk when he came home, went straight to the fridge and poured himself a glass, like a boy, and downed it breathlessly, adorning himself with a milk moustache. And when our father was tired he'd just flop on the sofa, sigh, his eyelids fluttered, and there he was fast asleep.

When Dad ate he stuffed his face. He ate like a horse, our thin father, dolloping in food with his lips the way a tinker's horse mouthed a carrot off your palm. But even that took too long, so he also shovelled his bangers and mash in with fork and spoon. Dad looked like he was force-feeding someone else's mouth, punishing them with meat and two veg. What it did to his digestion one can only imagine, as barely-masticated mouthfuls of food were packed off to his unfortunate gut.

THE OTHER week I plucked up the gumption to visit my young doctor, and confess the unease I'd been feeling lately.

'About your boy?' he asked. 'Surely not. Not now.'

'No, no,' I assured him. 'About myself.' I said, 'I get a prickling in my scalp. Also, in the skin of my thighs. Worst of all, on my back.'

'An itch?'

'I scratch at the isolated pinpricks, convinced it's just a couple of midgey fleas. You know the sensation? Like, on my legs. You lift your trousers and give the fleshy back of your calves a good scratch. Run your fingernails up and down the shin, where the skin's close over the bone. Or in there at the back of the knees. The relief.'

'Yes, yes, indeed.'

'Higher up, and you can scratch your legs through the material of your trousers or, in meetings, thrust hands deep into pockets and, surreptitiously . . .' I shrugged. 'Detected, the movement could be mistaken.'

'Quite.'

'You might attempt to squeeze your hands down between waistband and underwear and give a good scratch.'

'I see.'

'Of course, if I'm on my own, there's no problem. I undo

the trousers – take them off if I care to – and give myself over to a good bout of scratching.'

'Sounds reasonable.'

'But meetings, Doctor – that's the trouble. What do I do then? Discussions, chats, with however menial a hand. Meetings happen all the time. We employ three hundred people.'

'Here? No.'

'Of course not. I meant if you add up everyone all round the country. Yes, yes, including part-timers. Yes, and the migrant workers, of course, but there aren't many of them any more. Jobs, I mean, not migrants. More migrants than ever. More than we need. What was I saying?'

'Meetings?'

'A job interview, say, with some young applicant. I'm not one of those freaks, you know, those monsters.'

'I'm not sure I follow.'

'Megalomaniacs. Unlike my brother, I do try to accord every individual a certain respect. Even the lads we get.'

'Young men.'

'For washing, packing jobs. They sit there dumb. Dense. Marooned. No social skills, Doctor, I guess it's, oh, it's everything, isn't it? It's staring at a screen, it's absent fathers, it's that relish of ignorance in our working-class culture. Where's the vim of youth? The girls have it. Girls no longer teach themselves to be still. They're the ones with spunk now. Really. We recruit more women every year.'

'And in meetings?'

'What?'

'You were saying.'

'Yes, I was. Like, my hands, it's easy, I quietly rake them. Scalp too I can scratch openly, just taking care not to do so so often it attracts attention. But the back, Doctor. This is the problem. How can I reach my spine surreptitiously? You tell me. No, of course not. I can only suffer and squirm. If it's bad enough – and it can become unbearable – I've been known to excuse myself from meetings and rush to the toilet, there to wrestle jacket, tie, shirt from off my back and let myself loose in a frenzy of scratching.' I leapt up, shed garments, mimed. 'With pen, or keys, or – if I remembered in my agitated state to grab one on the way out – a ruler, acting as an extension of my arm and fingers so that I can stretch, you know, *contort*, and reach that unreachable spot, the inside of the shoulder blade there, where the insect loves to lurk.'

I sat back down, having gone to some trouble to suggest the full extent of my exertions. Got my breath back.

'Of course, there are no insects, as I am forced, each time it happens, to admit; as well as the fact that the itching is not on the skin, it's under it.'

The doctor nodded his head in that reassuring yet infuriating way of medical men.

'It's a non-specific itch?' he asked.

I smiled. 'A non-specific itch roaming around my body, Doctor.'

'Let me examine you,' he said.

T HE RING road curves ahead. I'm cruising along here and my mind turns over. My father. Me old dad: he was all nervy, a flurry of too many things to do, but he'd stop and puff himself up. Try and give an example. Think. OK. It's a Sunday morning. I'm thirteen years old. My mother asks over breakfast how I intend to spend my day. I say I'm not sure whether I want to go to my room, to do the homework I need to do before the end of the weekend, now or this evening.

My father considers this a moment, frowns across the kitchen table, nods gravely and – though I'd not asked for any response from him at all – says, 'Son. You do whichever you *feel* like doing.'

'Yes,' I say, 'I will.' It's not possible to say, *Of course* I'll do what I feel like doing. I, Dad. *Me*.

And a little later a neighbour will drop by and I'll overhear Mum tell her, 'The lad's in his room, studying. His dad told him to do his homework now instead of this evening, get it over and done with and out of the way, if that was what he *felt* like doing. So he's in there now.'

And my father, sitting by the fire, rolling himself a thin cigarette he'll take outside to smoke, frowns with smug sagacious modesty. The wise father.

I guess, looking back, my mother really was as stupid as

23

him. Dad's paternal authority was based on a weak impression of command, but it convinced Mum as well as himself. Well, he fooled me for a few years. I have a child's image of him discarding a finished cigarette: he held it between thumb and forefinger and he had a habit of flicking it away, into the mud, with great deliberation; with a flourish. An image from the years when I still loved and respected him.

In my memory our mum spent all day preparing the evening meal. That's all I see her doing: slowly washing, mixing, plucking, stringing it out like an old lag consigned to kitchen duties. Coping with the tedium by taking any excitement or creativity out of cooking, sliding into a trance.

'Always peel your potatoes in advance,' I can hear her advising her daughter. 'Save time later, Melody. Cut them up and leave them to soak.' Generations of women letting the vitamins in potatoes leach out.

Dad and I were doomed to fight. He always considered me lazy. He lacked the imagination to see that reading, and study, could demand intense and exhausting commitment. Because he in his time had idled through school, a prison sentence to be endured, he thought scholars were just people who actually enjoyed daydreaming. Dad lived in the body, expressing himself in action, and nothing else made sense.

When I look back now, what saddens me is that a lifetime's rumbling conflict was based on such an absurd misunderstanding. I try and tell myself that this is not possible, it's too pathetic to be true, that there was surely a genetic, a chemical, incompatibility between us. That in fact we were too alike, two tall, thin, clumsy men desperate to achieve what we set out to in this world. We were reflections of each other, Dad and I, distorting mirrors that showed us only our flaws.

Dad made fun of my reading and I fought him, and our love was fierce and tense and fluctuating. Mum supported me, always, and all I've had for her has been contempt, really, for the self-imposed limits of her existence. Now I can appreciate what it took to raise three children, the years of selflessness in which Greg and I and Melody could begin to grow in our own directions. But the brutal fact is that this recognition can't wipe away the derision that built up in my feelings towards her over so many years.

I do my best to love Mum, a dutiful middle-aged son, to play my albeit junior role to Greg and Melody in providing everything she needs in her gaping dotage, but it's too late for me to take my mother seriously.

Greg too was mystified by his younger brother's book-ishness. He was as sharp and jumpy as Dad on the stall: before he'd reached double figures Greg could haggle in a variety of styles, from flirtation to insult, generosity to pleading, according to what you deemed this or that customer was most likely to be seduced by. He could tot up running totals of this many strawberries and that much cabbage as he weighed them out; was able to file an interim figure on a little shelf in his brain if he needed to chat about the weather or invite the lady to give his ripe banana a prod any time she liked; and then, as soon as note or coins had changed hands, each sum was erased from Greg's mental slate.

I tried to learn from him. 'Like a teacher wiping the blackboard,' I ventured.

'No,' Greg frowned, slowly. 'Like a bookie,' he said.

On occasional Wednesday evenings we were invited to accompany Dad on his one and only hobby. The stadium was situated a few streets away from us. As well as dog racing, it also hosted speedway which, since it didn't interest Dad, Greg and I only ever heard: a whine, like a plague of angry motorbikes descending through the night sky, reached us in our beds.

'There's no pleasure in gambling on machines,' our father claimed. 'Think about it, boy.'

In the holidays Dad would tell Mum, as we sat around the dinner table, 'The lads can come to the track with me tomorrow night,' as if good and generous news was unmanly unless filtered through a woman.

'Why can't I come, Daddy?' Melody complained.

'You're too young!' Greg or I would authoritatively inform her. 'It's not for girls!'

But the satisfaction gained from this confirmation of our maturity was short-lived, since none of us could bear to see Melody disappointed, so the rest of the evening was spent competing with each other to promise her the best consolation.

'I'll take you tadpoling,' I could suggest.

'Let's go to the pet shop,' Greg would trump me, 'and watch the aquariums.'

Melody gave us her tolerant smile.

'Don't spoil her,' Mum said, and then, 'You can come shopping with me Saturday, love, and we'll have tea at Lyons.'

'We'll split our winnings with you,' Dad declared, which amused not only Melody but every one of us.

On the night of the dogs Dad would be involved in some odd-job or paperwork. The time Greg and I knew we ought to leave would come and be long gone when he'd abruptly drop what he was doing, bark, 'Jump to it, lads, we're late! On our way!' and stride out of the yard. Dad rolled and lit a cigarette as he marched, Greg and I lagging behind his brisk pace then scurrying to catch up, in children's awkward, unfair trot-walk.

In the executive lounge of the stadium fat and pallid

people in synthetic clothes sat in a gruesome wash of bright light and plastic, ate scampi and chips and sipped their beer or Babycham, and gambled in a polite manner. Not us.

We were out on the concrete terraces in a nervous crowd of men, up from the bookies leaning their black-boards against the fence along the home straight. If he remembered, Dad bought himself a pint of beer, and bottles of Coca-Cola with straws in for Greg and I. The floodlights made people who strayed into their glare too realistic. Dressed in cotton coats, dog owners paraded their hounds to and fro before each race. Fragile, tight bundles of springy sinew bred for brief speed, who'd been steered to an evolutionary fulfilment in this tedious, eternal, uncomplaining circling of race-tracks after a motorised hare.

The bookies stood with one hand on their board's shoulder, a stub of chalk and a duster in the other, and they kept stealing glances at each other's boards like girls at a dance.

Checking his competitors – 3–1 on here, on dog number three; 7–2 there – a tout erases figures and chalks up 4–1. Some of the punters were systematic gamblers who spread their bets in good time, but the ones you looked for and couldn't take your eyes off as the tension began to build before each race were the men standing at the back of the terraces to get a wide view of all the blackboards, the gimlet-eyed men, blinking less as a race approached, watching the bookies chalking and wiping and changing the odds. Men who'd forgotten to eat, and smoked their cigarettes hungrily. On the days he felt lucky, Dad was up amongst them. Men with beaked noses and unnatural stillness who ignored the dogs being gathered behind the starting cages, watched only the bookies' boards, the dusters and chalk, until, when the dogs were in and the gates about to be sprung, the men swooped down the terraces and swiped their wads of dosh all at the same tout, whichever one had outguessed his fellows with the best odds on offer at the last possible moment. Then the race shot off.

Here I am, tracing the ring road, as ridiculous as any greyhound. I'll turn off for work next time around.

I loved the dogs but I was frustrated by an inability to grasp the essential nature of the event, which Greg clearly got without having to try. It took me a while to even catch on that it was not about the dogs, the sport, the racing. It wasn't social, it wasn't the men or the beer. 'OK,' I told Greg, 'it's about the money. I can see that.' But I still couldn't. It was right in front of my eyes. I tried to work it out, to find the logic at the heart of it. The punters didn't care about the dogs, and neither did the bookies. They never even looked at the dogs until a race started. No one had superior knowledge of form, fitness, potential. The dogs were living dice thrown on to the track, their placings from race to race, week to week, almost entirely arbitrary.

'It's about the odds,' Greg explained to me when finally I asked him. 'Men put their money on the odds.'

Far from solving a riddle, Greg's lucid explanation only moved it further away, because the logic of the game is one men either feel in their guts or miss altogether. 'That means they've got no control,' I complained. I was nine or ten then, thirsting for clarity.

'I know,' Greg smiled. 'Gambling, John. It's great, isn't it?'

No, Greg wasn't stupid, not at all. He was a dab hand with a slide rule and he memorised half of his log tables. He did well at school, passed exams in almost every subject, but he left at sixteen to enter the family firm. For

Greg, school books and other ones were entirely utilitarian objects, their value measurable by the information they stored, their status as collectible items or, yes, he would accept, the pleasure they gave. 'Or insight, or understanding, or wisdom, John,' Greg would concede. 'Sure.' It was just that whatever qualities you said books possessed had to be at least theoretically measurable to make any sense.

Greg still sees things this way. If you tell him Lily took you to see the new film showing at the Paradise he'll say, 'Was it good? What do you give it, John? Marks out of ten?'

Our mother's timidity made her a detective. She had to construct portraits of people – not even their secret lives, merely basic facts about them – from the flimsiest evidence. Surveillance from behind net curtains, glances on the street. She hoarded these observations and what she deduced from them, and only brought them out in the open when she felt that we, her audience, were ready.

'You know that chap who moved in to the old house on the corner,' Dad said one dinnertime. 'With the Ford. Couldn't get it started this morning. He had to handcrank it, I haven't seen anyone do that in years.'

'Poor Mr Budgen,' our mother chose to contribute. 'I hope his hands were not harmed.'

A general mystified silence, expectant stares.

'Mr Budgen, I believe, is something of a musician.'

'He is?'

Our mother nodded sententiously. 'He was carrying a piece of sheet music under his arm the other day.' Turning to my brother and me, she said, 'If you see Mr Budgen struggling with his car again, boys, you might offer to help push-start it. Or get your father to fix up a tow. Mr Budgen is a sensitive man.'

Mum revealed in such moments of triumph only, in

reality, the paucity of her privileged information, and how negligible was her contact with other people. You understood at once she'd never exchanged so much as a word with Mr Budgen. Such moments provided also the closest she came to criticising our father, to engaging with him at any kind of contentious level – critical burrs which sailed right by him. The next time Dad, our uncouth, outgoing father, saw this Budgen character he'd be sure to greet him, 'How are you, mate? We heard that you tickle the old ivories.'

Let me admit something: I can be sly. Cunning. I observe things. I always have.

At the age of ten or eleven I noticed that our mother possessed a strange and furtive habit. After visiting the lavatory my mother, I began to notice, would worry that she hadn't flushed the toilet, and would return to check, invariably re-emerging a moment later without having had to do anything.

Over a period of days, I cottoned on to what Mum was doing. I'd hear the flush of the toilet and rush to the bathroom. If it was our mother who emerged I'd come up with a reason to stick close by her over the following minutes. Sure enough, she'd become oddly uneasy, and I do believe I knew why before she did. After a minute or two she'd stop what she was doing and return to ascertain she'd flushed the toilet or that the flush had actually carried away her effluent. I'd follow her at a distance.

This little routine – the creeping uneasiness, the compulsive return – was unvarying, yet no one else seemed ever to notice, which says a lot about Mum's low profile.

I never told her. I never told my brother, either, and already then I told Greg everything. I suspect Mum was only dimly aware of this habit of hers, or at least would have been shocked to be told that she did it every time she performed an evacuation of any kind – which she, after all, like the rest of us, did and does a dozen times a day. So I never told her. It was enough satisfaction to me, even then, to know. And, I confess, some part of my sly mind thought it might be useful to hold in reserve for a time when it might be needed. When I could use it against her.

Melody joined Greg and me helping Dad on the stall on Saturdays. 'My little customer magnet,' he called her, and he was right. People queued up to be served by Melody, and they were patient when she forgot the price of beans or had to call on Greg to help add up a convoluted order. But sometimes it wasn't so obvious, or focused, you just realised that the stall was pulling people towards it in a way that didn't happen when Melody wasn't there.

'Oh, she's so pretty, your girl,' frowning, middle-aged women told Dad, as if accusing him of obtaining her illegally, or as if her parents had contrived to somehow exaggerate her looks.

'She's such a pretty one,' they'd say to Greg or me, shaking their heads, as if to inform us, Aren't you lucky brothers? But also, Poor girl, poor father, poor family, what she, they, have in store. Foretelling a future, inevitable catastrophe. Which in a way, some might say, turned out to be the case. Though not me, oh no. Not me.

Years later, in therapy, to which I was referred by my GP in the hope of curing the depression that dogged me all through my twenties, the therapist did her best to convince me that the burial of envy of my older brother's attention, if not the denial of jealousy at a younger sister's arrival, had been devouring me all these years.

'Own your envy,' she urged me. She was a prematurely white-haired wise woman and she was all wrong for me. I divulged the information I felt I should, and had it turned against me. She had me make up stories. Strange spontaneous fairy tales emerged from my mouth. Out in her consulting room the oxygen of her, our, attention destroyed them. She seized upon disintegrating fragments.

'What does this figure, the simple-minded mother, mean? Why did you say that in those words?'

'It's fiction,' I said.

'Of course,' she said. 'What are our whole lives, if not fictional narratives? And where, if not in fiction, can we be our true selves?'

We discussed art, me the philistine merchant. Painting and sculpture. Yes, fruitseller, that's right, market-trader. People forget I went to university. A yow-yow barrow boy, living it up with the Hooray Henrys, the ya-yas and the la-di-das.

It's ironic, Greg and I were earning cash, real money, from early on, as soon as I joined him, during a period, in the late seventies, when the best art was critical of any kind of economic enterprise. Money was evil. I read novels, watched films, attended plays that inveighed against the iniquities being perpetrated upon society by men such as myself. Socially, people spat out the words *capitalist*, *bourgeois*, *liberal*, expelling dung-words from the sanctity of their mouths.

'Late Capitalism,' they'd claim, referring to the period we were then living through, 'has completed the transformation of works of art into commodities!'

How times change. Little did they realise it was – still is – Early Capitalism.

My therapist and I had fantastical conversations, as she sought the truth behind the fiction of a self I presented to the world. I was unhappy. *Why?* Women don't love me. *Did your mother love you?* Or is it that I don't love women? *Remember the mother figure in that story*

32

*you told me? Let us discuss her, no? I have some ideas about her.*

I wonder now whether my therapist was not a great and thwarted artist – in the same way that for a while certain critics saw themselves as artists. Or maybe, in fact, not thwarted at all. I mean, does art *need* an audience?

The therapist's only audience was the bringer of the material she worked with, the bearer of cargo. Her audience of one was also the canvas she worked on. Her form, and her content, were at the same time her living witness. Perhaps that was and is enough?

My therapist wasted weeks trying to persuade me I was in love with my mother – not that she believed it, it was merely a hypothesis that needed to be tested, but like an article of faith in gods or quarks I had to admit it in order for it to be tested in the first place. Yet she entirely overlooked the possibility that I might be in love with my sister. I'm not saying I am, but if the poor cow had asked to see the photos that I carry in my wallet of each member of my immediate family, man would she not have changed tack instantly? Watch that boom. Everybody duck. This boat is changing direction.

An abiding image I have of Melody is from when she was a teenager, fifteen or sixteen, at the pretty, lissom height of her loveliness: I was in town and I happened to spot her walking alone along the bustling High Street. Her dark lustrous hair, her Mediterranean complexion, her almond eyes. Aware of other eyes upon her. Perhaps most teenagers suffer a particular self-consciousness, this assumption that they are the centre of others' attention, but in Melody's case, it was true! She didn't hunch herself in, no, she still walked tall as she always did as a child, but I saw how she was both bashful and surprised by the head-turning,

33

stalk-eyed gawking she attracted, walking through the shopping passers-by.

That was it: my sister looked startled by her own beauty.

My favourite breakfast as a child was a fry-up. Looking back, it was the only meal Mum didn't boil or strain the taste out of. There's no cooking involved, is there? Unless you count the potato cakes, or croquettes as Mum called them. They had to be mashed and mixed and coated, though I don't imagine she added mace, nutmeg, even parsley.

Croquettes. I'd forgotten: Mum started giving all sorts of dishes foreign – French – names. Without changing the way she cooked them. 'Parisian potatoes,' she'd say as she plonked a plate of cubed chips on the table. 'Pommes Anna,' she said proudly as she cut into a splodge of spud it'd taken her hours to ruin.

It's a bad thing to be ashamed, isn't it? Shame has no place in the modern world. We want authenticity. The details betray us. Take Mum, who was brought up in the northern suburbs of Greater London, and had elocution lessons when young. Though not enough, not nearly. I believe some of the brighter girls in her class, no, more likely the best-behaved, had been awarded the prize of a few such lessons in which they were taught to mimic the vowel sounds of the upper middle class. *The rain in Spain*, and all that. *Four score poor Moors*. But the result in my mother's case is that she's sounded ever since like a mimic; her speech a never-ending pastiche. If a stranger overheard her talking to a person born and bred in the class she aspires to they'd be hard pressed to guess whether she was acting cravenly towards that person or parodying them.

Because certain vowels my mother exaggerates. *Corn*,

*dawn*, last in her mouth subtly longer than they should. She ends up speaking English, her mother tongue, sounding like someone incredibly close to conquering a foreign language. An immigrant into the middle class, not in it at all, not even in her own head. And one vowel sound above all betrays her estuarine origins: her elocution lessons must have been cut short before they got to *How now brown cow*. Instead of sounding haughty she pronounces that syllable like a cat's *miaow*. In a more self-confident woman such words could have remained as stubborn vestigial homages to her respectable working-class heritage. But not our mother.

My brother and I took on our father's, our own local, West Midlands accent. Greg's is almost as broad as I remember Dad's being, while mine has been neutralised by the company I've sought.

At school, in the neighbourhood in which we grew up, being a successful pupil automatically rendered you a suspicious alien, a clever dick, ripe for ridicule and bullying. This struck me as unfair, since I'd made no conscious effort to push myself forward to the front of the class. I simply wrote essays, handed in homework, sat exams, and tended to receive high marks.

Having Greg as an older brother shielded me from actual threat, but I could sense resentment. And whether it was this or merely the habit of working hard during my progress through Headley Comprehensive School, I gradually developed ambition. It kindled inside me, and it was stoked by a desire to grow out of our world, to see what lay beyond; to make my own mark out there, to build a home far grander than any prefab, to live and work well away from fruit and vegetables.

I woke up early – I was a light sleeper, and I think Dad made just enough noise to wake me when he drove out of the yard – and used to lie in bed thinking of the future, making plans at dawn. On the way to school I shared my dreams with Greg, and he told me his, which were the opposite of mine, and it must have been the sharing itself that made us respectful of each other's divergent journeys.

Greg set up a second stall as soon as he could drive, shortly after his seventeenth birthday. He drove a van to weekly markets in towns around about us. I knew Greg planned to expand the business, that he would work as hard as Dad but that he'd also employ other people – a tactic Dad regarded as reckless – buy more vans, maybe rent a shop.

I was fourteen when Greg left school, able to look after myself if necessary, and I'd begun to specialise in science subjects. I'd gained a year by the time I sat Chemistry, Physics, Maths and Biology A levels, in each of which I obtained grade As, and I was offered a scholarship by St Catherine's College, Oxford, to study Biological Sciences.

In that last summer vacation I worked for Greg. He'd transformed our yard with the erection of a new, airy, corrugated-iron shed, and he made me warehouse manager, taking deliveries from lorries and loading up the fleet of three vans Greg was already running.

'You're efficient, John,' he said on one of my last days. 'You know that? I'll be sad to lose you. You'll be wasted in laboratories.'

When I went up for the beginning of the first term I took fewer clothes and supplies and equipment than I needed, just as much as I could bear alone, so that I could travel by coach rather than accept a lift from father or brother and be driven in a *Sharpe's Fresh Produce* van. I arrived at university like a refugee.

At Oxford in the mid seventies a comprehensive school boy with a West Midlands accent was bound to be daunted by the privileged majority of his fellows. It wasn't that you suffered any kind of direct prejudice or snobbery. Some of those sons and daughters of the nobility, indeed, were the most graceful and generous companions I've known. It was just that they were changelings. In lectures, in the college bar, on the football pitch, we looked alike. But when you glimpsed them as dressed-up members of archaic clubs you'd not heard of, never mind been invited to join, enacting arcane rituals, or when they stood up in the Union and spoke without nerves, or drank champagne not Coca-Cola through a straw, or disappeared for Christmas in Switzerland. That's when you knew how charming they really were, it was you who was the clod-hopping imposter.

None of this mattered in the lab: a white coat offered anonymity and I lost myself in experiments and essays. The study of cells and genes, of organisms and populations. I was immersed in plant and microbial biology, in the analysis of complex systems, having proceeded to the Honour School of Botany after Prelims. The fact is, we were too busy for introspection, attending ten lectures a week, one or two tutorials, and practical classes. I devoured set reading and reference books, applied my brain to problem-solving exercises. I discovered, of course, that there were plenty of people as bright as and brighter than me. But I was undaunted, confident I could achieve whatever I wanted through hard work and willpower.

In the evenings I tried to drink, but soon learned that alcohol, as well as cigarettes, marijuana, amphetamines, were poisons inimical to my own biochemistry, for rare enjoyment only.

There were college discos. I can't dance and never could. I've always been one of those uptight men, who have to grit their teeth to get down on the dance floor. You have two options: stiff or floppy. You either do a kind of stilted jerk in one place, march on the spot until the time comes when it's not too shameful to slip away, or else you do what I do, which is to let yourself loose and let what happens to your body happen. The disco flop.

I had sex with four or five girls during my three years at Oxford without establishing a relationship with any one of them. My overriding impressions of those days are of hard work and solitude, less in the lab, focusing one's attention down the gaze of microscopes into the molecular structure of life, than out in the field: in Wytham Woods, the Botanic Garden and the Arboretum at Nuneham Courtenay.

I have a clear memory of sitting down in the St Catz bar one evening, exhausted with study, and taking a long draw from a pint glass of beer. I became aware of the alcohol floating through my blood, felt my eyelids flutter, and my brain begin to relax the tension holding it together. And I remember realising that, for all my supposed intelligence, I couldn't quite work out whether I was the happiest man alive or in a state of severe depression.

I completed Finals in the early summer of 1976, assuming – as did my tutors – I'd get a First and return to Oxford to study further, either by doing research towards a doctorate or by postgraduate training in Forestry. In my dawn plans, in a narrow bed in a shared house on Kingston Road, I was leaning towards a future concerned with natural resources in tropical countries.

Although in those days we received government grants that covered most of our living expenses, I'd borrowed some money from Greg, so without waiting for my results I went straight home to work for him. For *Sharpe and Son*, as Greg had generously renamed the company, although Dad ran just his one stall in town still, as he always had.

Actually, I discovered that Greg was having to cover Dad there with one of his employees, because Dad, who never missed a day's work, kept having to admit he felt too ill to lift crates. Always a thin man, he'd lost weight, and looked like the victim of some inexplicable assault. At supper he'd frown at the plate Mum put in front of him as if surprised by it. 'Not for me, love,' he'd tell her, and when he saw me looking at him, say, shaking his head in a puzzled way, 'I seem to have lost my appetite, son.'

Dad would get up from the dinner table and wander outside to have a cigarette and try and work out why he wasn't hungry, but you knew, really. His body was refusing sustenance, like he was living on smoke, and you knew.

'I've got a neat project for you, John,' Greg told me. 'I want you on the road.' There was a potato supplier in town who was about to retire, and Greg had bought the business. It was a small operation, consisting almost entirely of a contract to supply a few primary schools, and Greg pitched me right in: I spent my first week back home motoring round with Alfred Jemson in the green van he was bequeathing us, being introduced to various catering managers and dinner ladies. The following week Alfred was putting his feet up in Benidorm, while I drove the newly sign-written *Sharpe and Son* van from school to school.

It was the summer that changed my life. The work was a breeze. I started seeing a girl, Jen, one of Melody's friends who'd just left school. We went swimming in the warm evenings in the river north of town, I fed her ripe peaches, and we screwed on a rug in the grass or, when Jen's flesh goose-pimpled as the sun went down, in the earth-smelling back of Alfred Jemson's spud van.

All summer Dad was dying. When he went into hospital

we spent most of each Sunday up there, Mum and Melody camped by his bed. Greg would go outside for a smoke, and I went with him.

'Don't think I'm not proud of you, John,' Greg told me. 'I am, as much as Mum, or Melody. Dad too. But I do wish you'd join me.'

I was just as proud of Greg. He was barely twenty-three and already established, a man of substance in our town. We sat on the grass bank at the side of the hospital and gazed over the rooftops of the town spread out below. People walked to and fro, between hospital and car park, in front of us.

Greg stubbed out his fag and grabbed me, wrestled me down the bank and held me in a headlock. 'My little boffin brother,' he said, and kissed my forehead before letting me go.

'Jesus, Greg,' I said, picking stems of grass off my clothes. 'Look at this stain.'

We climbed back up the bank.

'I do wish you'd come and work with me,' Greg said. 'Don't laugh. I'm serious. It's lonely. I've got people work for me but they don't give a shit.'

'How many people now?' I asked him. 'Seven?'

'Eight. One's part-time, and one just a Wednesday.'

'Right.'

'I've got four vans. I've got three stalls, plus Dad's. I've got the schools contract. I've got the shop now.'

'Your first shop already,' I said, shaking my head. Dad had laboured thirty years with no thought of such progression.

'The overheads pile up like you wouldn't believe, John. I'm in debt up to here. I hate it. And all they want is to give you more. My bank manager says, "Come and see me, Greg. Whenever you need a further loan."'

'They're not stupid,' I said. 'He must know you're a good bet.'

'I can't stand to look at another business plan.'

I turned to smile at my brother. He looked like I'd never seen him before: angry, anxious and a little bewildered. 'I can't stand it.'

'This is not about Dad, is it?' I said. Greg didn't respond. We sat in silence for a while. 'Oh, it must be,' I declared, leaning forward and letting gravity bring me to my feet, and I pulled Greg up. 'Come on, brother, let's get back in there. He'll be all right. Dad's a fully paid-up member of the awkward squad: he'll be on the stall next week just to wrong-foot you.'

My older brother has been a big and bluff and reassuring presence all through my life. I grew up with it and it's there with me today. People respect and trust Greg. He's afraid of no one. But for that brief moment, a couple of months, what he'd built was trembling. I couldn't admit there was something, everything, he couldn't handle. I resisted my own awareness that Greg had reached his limit, his own glass ceiling. Indeed, he was already over-extended. The fact was, Greg had no gift for abstraction. As long as he could see what he owned, count the turnover in his head, watch what his employees were doing, haggle and barter, juggle the components of a business like oranges in his hands, then Greg was the master of his domain. But the business was spreading around and beyond him and he was lost.

The following Sunday we sat on the same brown sun-baking grass outside the hospital. 'It's not difficult to begin to analyse a complex system,' I told him. 'And this is a simple one. All you want to do is systematise the processes involved.'

'I do wish you'd join me,' Greg said gloomily. Then he

brightened. 'Could you do that this summer, John?' he asked. 'This analysis of yours?'

My degree result came. I opened the envelope in the yard and stared at the piece of paper, not breathing. They hadn't given me a First. They'd given me a worthless 2:1. 'A good 2:1, John,' my tutor would bullshit me, a couple of days later. It was the mark of bright youth. Of clever students who'd spent their time in drama or sport or debate; of future politicians, journalists, businessmen, who'd go on to run the country. Intelligent people who had things in perspective.

A good 2:1 was the mark of the not quite Firsts, the almost geniuses but not really. In fact, nowhere near. Actually also-rans. The workaholics for whom no amount of study and revision could make up that gap between themselves and those destined for profound academic success.

Realising my knees were about to go I sat on a crate in the yard, put my head in my hands. Melody came out with a glass of water. 'Are you OK?' she said. 'You're shaking.'

'I'm fine,' I said.

'What happened? Did you faint?'

'Of course not.'

'You're white,' Melody said.

I was struggling not to weep. 'Piss off,' I said.

There was silence. It was the only time I've ever spoken like that to Melody.

'I'm going inside now,' she said. I glanced up. She was smiling at me. She turned and went away.

It took me another two days before I could tell anyone. Two days of coming to terms with betrayal: I couldn't work out why I'd been deceived, and deceived myself. I'd thought I could do and have anything I wanted, but it turned out this wasn't the case. A small knot of rage tightened in the pit of my stomach. Who knows? Maybe it's still there today.

Of course, when I told my family, they were delighted with my degree. Greg broke open a bottle of Asti Spumante around Dad's bed, and Dad promised he'd be out of hospital for my graduation.

'I don't intend to miss you in a black gown, Johnny,' he said, spluttering with feeble laughter. 'And a plasterer's board on your head.'

They were almost his last words to me.

We're coming up to Kite Hill. Up there's the hospital. There on that floor's the ward where we visited him. He never believed he was dying. The weaker he got, the more tubes and wires his wasted body was tethered by, the more plans he made. No one told him. They do things differently now. He was withering in front of our eyes and he started croaking at Mum about holidays, taking her abroad. Childhood summers once or twice he drove us down to Weymouth. Mum didn't want to go anywhere but Dad acted like she did and always had, like he'd make it up to her as soon as he bounced out of that hospital bed.

Mum'd have a sob once we got out in the echoey corridor. 'Majorca,' she'd say. 'Dad wants to take me to Majorca,' she sniffled in the car on the way home from watching the cancer consume him, right there in front of her.

We want to live long. We want our children to live for ever. To be spared death. A chap I know has a company developing xenotransplantation: the transfer of animal organs, hearts, kidneys, livers, into human beings. Humanised pigs. Genetically altered to match an individual

43

client, ready and waiting to provide an organ when those of that person fail.

Certain primitive tribes believe themselves watched over by unearthly guardians: each soul accompanied by an animal familiar. Eagle, panther, gorilla of the spirit world.

Now my son too will be protected, by his very own lab animal.

# Blight

Haulm: Initially brown spots with
pale green margins, often with
whiteish mould on undersurface.
Spread can be rapid with leaves
killed completely.

Tubers: Brown to purplish areas on skin,
with rusty-brown, granular
marks in the flesh.
May remain dry and firm, but often
followed by soft rots.

# MONDAY 10 A.M.

WILL THEY say that I am implicated?
There were four people in the control group. Two of them are fine. They had diarrhoea, vomiting, some sweat and shakes, but now they're recovered. The two unfortunate specimens who died were ill-chosen: one too young, the other too old. Their selection by the scientists in the field was irresponsible, not to say reckless. It may be that Simon and I should inform some authority of the scientists' error before they return. Yes, this may well be the thing to do.

I'm driving around the ring road. Here comes my exit again already. Time to turn off: apply your fingers to the indicator. Their weight is not enough to depress it. They tremble. Oh, look, I missed it.

Cobditch. Buckland. Foxmoor. There's the crematorium. They're always out of town, aren't they, crematoria? Yes, Lily, I got it right. That's the plural.

The priest at the crem, a stranger to us all, gave a short eulogy gleaned from what we'd told him about Dad. Worker, joker, abiding husband, pillar of his community, stalled in the market thirty years. He summed Dad up well in a few words. Then he said, 'Let us pray.'

People had already stopped kneeling, hadn't they? We

47

don't want to be disrespectful to ourselves. There was a sound of bottoms shuffling as people sought a compromise: we leaned forward; we ducked. I glanced behind me. Mourners trying to hide. From the priest? From God? I don't know.

What can you do? You take a bit of Celtic myth from here and a bit of Hindu yoga from there, as Lily does. It's either that, or ignore the whole business, like me. I don't see what else you can do.

Many years later, long after Dad's death, I spotted him and Mum crossing the High Street. It had only just been pedestrianised. Dad looked surprisingly spry, although both my parents appeared suspicious of the vacated tarmac. Hand in hand Dad was helping Mum, leading the way, but he looked as anxious as she did as they made their tentative way across a road in which there was no traffic. Their every step suggesting unseen dangers which might have *replaced* traffic, and could erupt in front of them, an invisible obstacle course.

And it was many more seconds, half a disbelieving and wonderful minute, before I understood that it wasn't Dad at all, it was some other thin man crossing the road with Mum. In fact, it wasn't even Mum. It was two strangers my brain mixed up, in a moment of derangement, with my parents.

When I was a child we were given polio vaccines in a sugar cube. All others were by injection. There was no doubt which we children preferred.

It's now twenty years since foreign DNA was first inserted into the genomes of plants. Shortly after that, it occurred to a couple of American molecular biologists that plants might be coaxed into expressing vaccine antigens, and eaten as an alternative to a jab.

This is the idea. Edible Plant Vaccines.

I met Simon Wright, the MD of AlphaGen, five years ago. I joined his board soon after. With academic partners in Plant Biology at Cambridge, AlphaGen had just achieved the first successful expression of a hepatitis vaccine in transgenic potato. They were almost ready to conduct human trials, and a partner in the potato trade – one willing to invest – was welcomed.

There can't be many ring roads go right around an old town like ours, roundabout to roundabout.

How nice it is to orbit the town. I wonder whether I or the car might get dizzy, going round in circles like this? I should cross to the other side, and resume in the opposite direction.

I feel like a satellite. Things are slowing down. We're gradually transcending the gravitational pull of the earth. Entering galactic time, where nothing matters if it lasts for less than a million years. Where empires rise and fall in the blink of an eye. Where all that matters is an ice age . . . or a falling star . . . or the birth of a child.

While my son sleeps beside me in the early morning, I scribble. I still make plans at dawn.

He doesn't like to be watched in his sleep, John Junior – which is what I call Jacob. He's like me (of course). However silent I am, he'll stir, he'll fidget. Sometimes his eyes open simply because, it seems, he's being observed. It's true, they really do. But I love to watch him. It feels less the absorbing observation of a process taking place, of life unfolding (though it is this too), than me feeding myself, visually. Feasting on my son with my eyes.

Our son is woken in the early hours, either by what Lily takes, from his reddened cheeks and drooling, to be teething, for which she slips a camomilla homeopathic pill on his tongue, or else by some hindrance in his digestion.

His mother soothes him with soft stroking words, but sometimes he won't be calmed and I scoop him up out of bed, rush him away from my exhausted wife. Then you may find me in the dead of night, feeding John J., my finger dipped in dill water.

His existence revolves around his digestion. Mysterious rumblings emanate from deep in his little gut; I listen to them like sonar readings, though I understand nothing. When his digestion upsets him he flexes and twists, grimaces, whimpers. Distressed by food – the processing of it or his need for more of it. Not in a minute or two or ten. Now!

I keep digressing. But I want to go over it all, everything, before I see my brother – so I can start explaining it to him.

I mean, Greg, look at where we are, I'll say. The Age of Enlightenment is dead. Civilisation didn't lead to ever greater civility, tolerance, equality. It was never going to – only over-educated fools thought so. No, we're back in the jungle. Or rather, the laws of the jungle operate up here on the high plain.

This is an age of reason. There's no religion, no ideology, no ideal, to inhibit us. Only relative secular humanism, and what does that amount to? If you can afford it, you can have it, you have a right to it. Everybody wants the money, so they can buy what they want. The only barrier to whatever we want is public opinion, a cautious, slow-moving animal, to be dragged along in the wake of brave pioneers.

Now our father was dead, I realised I need no longer situate myself in opposition to his determined ignorance. He wasn't there any more. And neither had Greg's business any connection to Dad's market stall other than a sentimental one.

'OK, Greg,' I said, at the end of that summer. 'I'll work with you.'

'You will? Really?'

'Partners.'

'Of course,' he said. 'That's what I'm offering, John. In everything.'

What was odd was that as soon as I made the decision I felt less that I'd given up one course of action – in science, in academia – than that I'd rediscovered a path allowed to grow over and obscured. As kids Greg and I helped Dad evenings, weekends and holidays, scaffolding the stall, humping crates. Me replenishing fruit displays, loudmouth Greg hawking raucous and unflagging.

My brother's hot; he grabs an orange and steps behind the back of the stall. Greg peels the orange salivating; as soon as he's peeled enough he plunges his impatient mouth in, greedy teeth puncturing tiny sacs, juice squirting out and dribbling down his chin, which he retrieves with his tongue. And, afterwards, after he's devoured the orange, ripping it apart and pulling off the last of the pulp clinging to the pith on the inside of the skin, Greg wipes his mouth with the back of his hand with so relishing a gesture that it looks like he's gained a further tangy pleasure from the act.

There was this one day, wasn't there, aged fourteen, when I stumbled upon a truth I think our dad sensed only dimly, if at all. Which was the sheer ubiquity of food. That everyone eats. A lot. We eat and drink, and we piss and shit. The delicious, fundamental basis of life, of human lives, meant that we were blessed, in the provision of food, not simply with the most necessary profession but an almost holy vocation. I remember this revelation, conferred upon me in a moment of grace.

Or was it a fortuitous whim of conversational flow?

Yes, that's more likely it.

One summer Sunday our father had dropped Greg and me off in a lay-by with a parasol, a crate of punnets of raspberries and strawberries, and a satchel of coins.

Hot tarmac. Petrol haze. I watched cars pass by. I served those travellers who paused to buy in a dozy, preoccupied manner. The cars went past, an eternal cavalcade, endlessly replenished. I began to think of the cars as like food, items of food endlessly conveyed. I thought of food as a flow of matter, and we, our bodies, enter that flow, let it flow through us, for the brief duration of our lives.

I mixed up someone's change, and when they'd gone my brother said, 'You're not with it.'

'I'm considering things,' I said.

'Get a grip, John.'

'These people.' I gestured with a sweep of my lower arm at the traffic. Swishing to and fro. 'What do they have in common?'

'They dislike public transport?'

'All these people,' I said. 'They're different. Young and old, kids in the back, men, women, white, black, rich or poor. Everyone different, but any of them might stop for a berry because they all eat.'

'Sure.'

I said it again. 'They all eat. Everyone.'

My brother stared at me. Then somehow he was staring in my direction but at me no longer. Greg looks down-right stupid when he's thinking. 'They all eat,' he said eventually.

'That's right.'

'Everyone eats.' He came over and placed his hands on my shoulders, looked into my eyes. I nodded. 'And we, John,' he said, 'we sell the food. If we do it right, we can't lose.'

Six years later came that summer that changed my life, the

summer of 1976. Three things happened: our father died, I failed to obtain the degree I expected, and it was the worst drought for a generation. People recall the heat but no one remembers that before the drought, in late May, even in some places early June, a late frost had fallen. It was a double whammy, the frost as much as the drought. Greg had already started dealing directly, on a very small scale, with a few potato farmers kind of inherited from Alfred Jemson. Come harvest, farmers who expected ten ton of spuds an acre were lucky if they got five; prices soared, and some of them got greedy. Desperate. They broke contracts they'd sealed with a handshake months before, demanding higher prices per ton for their diminished yield. Greg could see their point of view, and was prepared to haggle his way to a reasonable medium, but I told him we couldn't accept that.

'Trust me,' I said. 'Let me deal with this.' I said to our farmers, me twenty-one years old, 'You take the price we shook on; we're not paying a penny more. And if you break this deal, my brother and I'll never buy from you again.' Four farmers walked away, fetching better deals elsewhere.

We had to scratch and scrabble through the following winter, rustling up spuds wherever we could to keep ourselves and one or two other retailers we began to work with supplied. We even hustled old guys on their allotments to sell us a few tatties. But our reputation was made. Farmers knew we'd strike a deal and stick to it, and they came to us.

We never did do business again with a single one of those growers who reneged that summer. Greg and I toasted the last of them to sell up, around 1993, as I recall. We happened to be driving past this bastard's small farm soon after hearing the news and Greg pulled the car over in a gateway. We walked into a field, unzipped our flies and pissed on his last lot of haulms. Our own triumphant crop spray.

My word is my bond.

No, that's not quite true, is it? Like, for example, just now, I confess, I made that up about a therapist. Would I have lain down on the couch of some old Jung witch and bared my soul? Am I serious? With my background?

Business plans may have made Greg anxious, but I saw them as absolutely necessary. I spent my first months working with him, with *Sharpe Brothers*, analysing the business we had and that we might hope to develop. Greg and his team were quite capable of running things as they were so, appropriately enough, the boffin brother studied. I read. I attended conferences and seminars. I spoke to management consultants, bank managers, agriculturalists, retail advisers, wholesale experts. I outlined plans, sketched flow charts, drew up columns of speculative figures. I stared at a pocket calculator Greg gave me, adding and subtracting endless variables.

Above all I woke at dawn every morning and made myself a cup of tea and returned to bed. If occasionally there was a girl there, Jen having moved on, I'd do my best not to wake her, and lay in the dark, thinking. That was where I let what I'd learned sink in and make clear to me its practical application. The following spring I laid out my plans for Greg. It was a short speech, that stunned him, for maybe a full minute, which is a long time when you're waiting for someone to say something. Then Greg shook himself and leapt to his feet.

'Sell the stalls?' he demanded, pacing the room. 'Even Dad's?'

'Yes,' I nodded. 'Let the guys you've got take them over if they want, pay us off in instalments.'

'Sell the shop?'

'That's right, Greg. Sell the lease outright.'

'But keep the school contract?'

'Hustle for more. Any way we can.'

He stopped prowling the room. 'And did you say? Am I right?' Greg peered at me. 'You're saying get rid of fruit and vegetables?'

'Except potatoes. Everything else.'

'Keep the warehouse.'

'Of course. Get Mum out of that trailer, we buy her a bungalow. We get rid of the trailer, and build more warehouse in the yard.'

Greg stood there, staring at the carpet, muttering, 'Get rid of the fruit and veg.' As if I'd mortally insulted Dad's memory. Shaking his head. 'Fruit and veg.'

Then he blinked at me, and said, 'Potatoes, John. Who knows? It might just work.'

'Trust me,' I said. 'It will.'

Is that the whole answer, though – economics? Is that why we specialised in potatoes? Or was it also because they're wondrous? You can't expect people to understand. Few do. But what I learned during those months is that what the Spanish brought to Europe towards the end of the sixteenth century can provide, supplemented with a single beaker of milk, a nutritionally complete diet. One acre of spuds provides more than ten people with their annual energy and protein needs, which is not true of rice or wheat, or corn or soybeans, or any other staple.

And what else? Their versatility. People may have seen the slogan a few years back: *You Can't Beat 'Em, But You Can Fry 'Em.* Variations on this were posted in supermarkets everywhere. *You Can't Beat 'Em, So Why Not Mash 'Em?* Yes, and *Boil 'Em. Roast 'Em. Bake 'Em.*

Greg claims he thought those up, doodled on his hand-held computer in a BPC meeting, downloaded to someone there. Swears it. I don't believe him, mind. But what other food can you do so much with? I can't name one.

*    *    *

The potato was brought to England by one of Elizabeth's marauding adventurers, Raleigh or Drake or Hawkins, in the late sixteenth century, but it took another two hundred years for the potato to take hold here. In the early days they were poor yielding, unreliable, susceptible to all kinds of disease and infection. But the beginning of the nineteenth century saw a string of poor cereal harvests: grain prices soared, and the Corn Law of 1815, which protected corn growers by restricting imports, kept them high. Riots took place, with the Napoleonic Wars going on in the background.

The government saw the result of dependence on one major food, and identified the potato as a cheap, alternative source for the masses. Parish officers were encouraged to provide allotments for the poor, which became known as potato patches.

The potato market, the amount consumed, increased enormously through the nineteenth century, eaten by the new class, the urban poor. They were hurried, overcrowded, and lacked equipment, fuel and time for cooking. Urban workers lunched on a mess of potatoes, into which a little butter or lard was poured, with fried bacon added occasionally. They dined on tea and bread. And in cities the baked-potata man appeared, a vendor who paid a baker to bake his spuds then sold them, with butter and salt, from tall cans kept warm with a charcoal boiler.

Potatoes as convenience food for the urban working class. A person could guess what came next: baked-potata sellers in Lancashire branched into frying at about the same time – the 1880s – that the steam trawler netted large catches of fish from ever further afield, to be rushed in ice on trains to inland markets. Fish and chips were married in a million plates of paper and greasy fingers.

And then there was war; war is always good for the food business. Gives us back our home market.

In 1914 Britain started out anticipating a swift and decisive campaign: little was organised in the way of food supplies, even though before the war already 80 per cent of our cereals were imported. Almost half our meat. Most people can't believe that, but it's true. By the winter of 1916, with German submarines taking a heavy toll of supply ships, potatoes as well as other basic commodities were limited and expensive – and that year brought, in addition, a disastrous harvest. As a result the government ordered increased acreage, high-yielding varieties and maximum retail prices, and production almost doubled in two years.

It was the same in World War Two – incentive payments to growers to increase their acreage, and fixed retail prices to encourage the public to consume this home-produced food – over the course of which production doubled. The Ministry of Food issued propaganda exhorting people to *Dig for Victory*. Women turned over their absent husbands' lawns and planted spuds. Local authorities converted parks into fields and roadside verges into long ribbons of allotments.

When I told Lily about Britain's wartime effort she pointed out that it was probably the digging, as much as the eating of what was dug, that made our nation healthier then than ever before or since.

Some mornings when I get to the office before anyone else I head over to the old aircraft hangars. We moved to the World War Two base beyond the common, and converted the hangars into purpose-built stores with forced crossflow ventilation and refrigeration systems, in 1983. I'd persuaded Greg the cold winter before, '82, or was it '81? Cost us a crippling amount of money, a loan I begged the bank for. Went down on my hands and knees. A crazy expense. One of the best things we ever did.

Our storage units in the old place couldn't cope that cold winter. The cheap heaters over-compensated, turned the warehouses into saunas, made the spuds perspire like Swedes, as Greg put it. Outside, the world froze, while inside those large units, a thousand tons of Pentland Squire and Maris Piper sweated away. Condensation dropped off the ceiling, down the sides, dripped off everything. Got into the control boxes, blew them off the walls.

So, anyway, what I do is when I get to work early, when there's no one around, I wander into one of the hangars. Leave the lights off, let my eyes become accustomed to the dark, and you know, I just breathe. Stand surrounded, and dwarfed, by tall columns made up of crates of potatoes. The smell's so strong it's like being in the lair of some underground animal. I inhale the dank and lovely smell of potatoes. Of the female, musky earth.

Greg is more primitive than me. He's more straightforward. I remember when our sister was fourteen or fifteen and in the first full bloom of her beauty, Greg, four years older, wanted nothing so much as the chance to protect her, to defend her honour. Melody's Botticelli beauty called forth such valour from him, from his deepest instincts, although in fact hers was not the sort of beauty that men lusted after. They were more likely to want to fight my brother for the privilege of protecting her! Hers was not that ripe fuckable loveliness of certain nurses, waitresses, secretaries in their make-up, their discardable uniform, sheer hose, rip-me panties, that a man may, if he is fortunate, stumble into in his fumbling way through this life.

No, Melody's beauty was pure. It inspired in regular men noble desires, chivalric tendencies lying dormant in their genes; it revitalised courtly dreams. Only irredeemable oiks and thugs, evolutionary waste washed up in our town, lusted after our sister with lewd gestures, Neanderthal propositions. These hooligans my brother fought.

Greg was impulsive, headstrong. Within years, if not months, of moving to the air base – *Sharpe Brothers* renamed *Spudnik* – we were employing almost a hundred people. Greg was dynamic, and in those early years it was his aggressive energy that animated our workforce.

My brother shouts at people. I never shout at people. How often I've had to intervene over the years! To assuage ruffled feathers in the pub, to calm sobbing girls at work, to part punchers. I am slow, ungainly, in my movement; I lurch, frankly, and look fondly down at the world from my unimposing height. But parting punchers at least is something tall men do best. What's the secret? Blocking eyelines is the secret. If you can stop two fighters eyeballing each other you've got a chance of neutralising the psychosis. It's a good tip.

I find fighting undignified, degrading. It's more natural for short men, close to the ground. We tall thin men are clumsy, absurd fighters. We lose our balance, become tottering, ineffectual dolts.

My brother is drawn to conflict. I am repelled by it. And I'm not one of those people who nurse grudges, while Greg blows up but then it's over. No, not at all. Me, I forget, while he'd gladly fight the same battle all over every day. I regard myself as tolerant. I accept oddity; flaws. A couple of years ago I was asked by a *Chronicle* journalist, for a full-page profile of a prominent local figure – which Lily tore out of the paper and Blu-tacked to the wall of the downstairs loo – what I would like for my epitaph. A rather morbid question, I thought, but I said, How about, *He suffered fools gladly*?

\*    \*    \*

59

It doesn't take much imagination to see why Greg and I made good business partners. I am cautious, thoughtful. I brood over the company's prospects, and plan ahead. People know that, both within *Spudnik* and outside. Anyone who wants to discuss the future knows to come to me. Because I manage. I sit down with the figures, and I work out the budgets.

Greg thinks on his feet. Bluff, blarney, bullshit. Which seems to be a necessary talent for managing human beings. For inspiring them. The ideal life for my brother would be one filled with brainstorming sessions: bored by his own company, he requires other people to ask questions he doesn't ask himself, to activate his brain. And when he's excited, other people get excited. I've seen it.

It was me who came up with the maxims for which our company gained a little satirical, useful publicity some years back – GROWTH = NATURE people sometimes remember; FOOD = THOUGHT – that we had printed not only on posters but on notepaper, letterheads, free stickers for our workers. Fridge magnets for our customers to take home and give to their kids. Greg had nothing to do with them.

I am remote. I don't have friends, for example. People like or dislike my brother. They care what he says to them. They're wary of Greg, but only in the most obvious way. When I think of each employee we've sacked over the years, I've been the one who dealt the fatal blow. It was principally my decision, and me who said the words: *I'm sorry, we have to let you go.*

One night, two or three years ago, my wife sensed me awake beside her at two in the morning. I'm never insomniac. I sleep soundly, but not this night. No idea why. No reason. Anyway, Lily asked what was wrong,

60

and I thought quickly, and I told her how the next morning I was going to have to tell this chap who'd been with us five years, on the graders, that he was no longer wanted. He had a young family, mortgage, the works, and I was certain he had no idea of what was about to befall him. But I explained to Lily how each time we updated machinery labour costs rose, and I'd considered this fellow's virtues and his failings and stared at my budgets, and I could not justify his salary.

As I told Lily all this I became quite emotional. I could tell it impressed her. Lily distrusts the rough and tumble of money, and the catch at my throat was something she was gratified to hear.

'I have to do it,' I said. 'Once I've done it, I'll be all right. But I don't like what I have to do.'

Lily gave me a sleepy kiss. 'Don't change,' she said.

Greg and I have always talked. We discuss everything, endlessly. I'd be quite happy to make big decisions alone, and I do believe Greg would let me; while I don't really need to know every detail of each conversation Greg's had with farmer, wholesaler, greengrocer and so on and on. But we yap and yak, and I think the words are the bricks in our relationship, they help to make us as formidable as we are. People know how different we may be but they also understand we're an unbreakable pair.

Even today, though, Greg gets fed up with admin-istration, and marketing, and I'll catch sight of him striding across the yard, pulling on a white coat and a hard hat. I know what he's doing. What he's doing is he's going to spend a couple of hours checking machinery and the men and women who operate it. He's going to make sure that two samples are taken off every load that's driven in, to be washed and assessed for temperature, mechanical damage and disease; he'll check that the hot-box, which accelerates their development so they can be tested again, is fine-tuned. He'll check the decanting of spuds from bulkers to boxes and he'll scramble over the Acupack, where the potatoes jiggle along riddles that grade them by size. 'They look like they're marching,' my brother'll tell someone, probably Frank, whose domain it is and has been ever since we installed it, the first in this country; who'll reply, 'Yes, boss, they do.'

Greg'll watch the women sorting the line and make sure they're picking out every reject for stock feed; he'll stare at the bagging machines that swallow punnets with thick clingfilm, and he'll scrutinise the girls sticking labels on bags for our supermarket customers. And you can be sure that he'll find mistakes, human and mechanical, wherever he goes.

'That bloody belt's out of alignment,' Greg'll shout. 'Those should be plastic, not wire, those screens.' Or, 'No, that's not how you do it, Jesus, give it here, I'll show you.' As long as they don't argue he'll hold nothing against anyone, and he'll come back to the office refreshed, content, spent.

When Greg swears at our employees they don't, on the whole, mind. He's yelled and cursed and even struck people. But as a result, when he compliments someone they know it means something. They glow. When my brother smiles with appreciation *their* faces light up too. They'll do anything for Greg, our workers, it's one of the secrets of whatever success we've had so far. The farmers we deal with, too. Whatever the state of things, Greg assures me, farmers don't want traders to share their misery: they want someone to turn up and tell a filthy joke or two, take the mick out of their rustic clothes, share some gossip. He's right.

* * *

I used to wonder of other people how they could waste their lives. I was bemused by those without ambition, droning out of school with neither skills nor plans. *How can you waste your life?*

Greg and I used to refer to such of our contemporaries as losers, wasters, riffraff. People who had no drive, would never amount to anything, whose entire working lives would depend upon the whim of ruthless bosses, the caprice of market forces. Youngsters like us, they were, with the same fresh sap in them but no, all they possessed was the vague expectation, or demand, that they'd be enveloped in the security of some mundane job, a career even, that would fill the dead hours of the week in which a human being was obliged to work and leave them free, with a little cash in their pocket and spring in their step, to enjoy the weekend. That was all.

When Greg and I began to employ other people, the losers, the wasters, began to work for us. They began to waste their lives doing our bidding, and I realised that this must have been what they were for: their function was to work for us, to help us build our little company.

Sometimes you learn true things about people that jolt your idea of them, that startle your framing of the world. Personal things. Secrets. Intimate trivia.

Take Greg. I know his opinions, his values. So many conversations down the years. Offer me any issue, I believe I could predict his response to it as well as I could my own. I know he thinks for example that *in vitro* fertilisation – though it failed Lily and me – is going to revolutionise the way we reproduce. And very soon. That his children, or certainly his grandchildren, will freeze their sperm and eggs early on and, while they then get sterilised and enjoy promiscuous lives, babies will be conceived in the lab.

And in the future, when someone wants to bring up a child, he or she will choose to mate their genes with those, yes, of their partner of the moment, perhaps, but possibly a friend with fine qualities. A good-looking neighbour, maybe. Or they'll pay for the DNA of some athlete, or actor, whoever they can afford.

'A thousand offspring of Britney Spears roaming the planet,' my brother conjectured.

I've not told him everything about me and Lily, but that's what he thinks. I know that. It is more personal details that surprise. A year ago Greg told me that he hated making love in bed. I wasn't sure I heard him right.

'A bed's for sleeping,' he maintained. 'I like sex in any other room. In *every* other room. In the hallway. On the stairs.'

My brother's marriage was long since over but he's a serial monogamist: he likes his life shared, in a committed relationship. When it turns, as it always does, he lets it go and gets quickly into the next one.

'What about first thing in the morning?' I asked him, playing for time. 'Don't you ever wake up with your woman, and you both kind of ease sleepily into each other?'

'Maybe,' he conceded.

At the time he was telling me this, Greg's girlfriend was a hazel-headed, energetic solicitor, with whom he disappeared at weekends to go sailing, often with a boatload of other rustling, laughing people.

'That heavy-lidded half-awake sensuality. She snuggles up to you. Don't tell me you yell at her, *No! Not here. Not in bed. Come to the kitchen. Let me ravish you upon the Formica work surfaces.*'

'OK,' my brother accepted. 'You pedantic twat.'

'*I demand the indentation of the draining board in your buttocks!*'

'Enough already. If I wake up and she's already cuddled up in the way you're describing, nuzzling into me, of course. What, am I going to spoil that? I'm telling you what I prefer, John. I prefer it in the bathroom. In the shower. The feel of porcelain.'

I sensed myself becoming aroused. I couldn't help imagining his breezy girlfriend, her flesh spread on white tiles, under running water, drops of water settling across her wide shoulders, on her diminutive breasts.

'I like it in the car, still,' he continued. 'I mean, am I a kid? No. But it makes me feel good.'

'You're a pervert,' I told him.

'And I like it up against the front door,' he said. 'I love that.'

'What? On the outside?'

'Inside, you moron,' Greg laughed. 'But of course it helps if someone comes up the garden path and knocks. Even better.'

John Junior has ready-made mentors, unfortunately: his cousins. Greg's sons are now aged fourteen and seventeen, and they sometimes come out to our place. It's very odd. I don't really know why they come. They seem to like Lily. They're street kids, townies, yet they get themselves a lift to the village and mess about on my quad bike, wheeling around the wild bit Lily calls our orchard. She can't watch.

'They'll kill themselves,' she says.

The older boy, Clint, lobotomises himself fiddling with his Game Boy. That frenetic docility, it disturbs me. He speaks reluctantly, in a little-used voice of grinding glass. Neither he nor Lee read, I don't know whether or not they can. Though they're never without a shiny and expensive magazine or two. Skateboarding. Techno. Football. As far as I can tell from cursory flick-throughs, these mags contain nothing but adverts, no editorial content whatsoever, nothing that demands more than two seconds' reading of words, nothing to interrupt the grazing over merchandise. Remarkable marketing, it really is. It makes sense: the boys are contented consumers. What would they rather browse than glossy enticements to consume more of their favourite products?

The boys can both loll for hours in our swimming pool. Mostly, though, they mooch around inside, moon in my wife's direction, gawk at our flat screen, gas plasma technology TV. Most of the time they live with their mother, some with their father. One gets the feeling they don't mind which but they'd prefer somewhere else again, really. Their own den to vegetate in.

The older boy (we seem to be a male-producing family; my sister remains the anomaly even through another generation) is as tall as me. Clint has a curious way of walking: he slouches while at the same time rising up off his tiptoes as he walks. He is a head taller than his father; towers above his mother. On the rare occasions that I see all four of them together, Clint makes Greg look, somehow, like a superseded model. Which I suppose he is. And I guess my own baby son will soon enough do the same to me. Hell, he already has.

We've developed *Spudnik* over the years slowly but remorselessly, and Greg has accepted all my plans. But he still doesn't quite trust genetic modification. He'd prefer us to concentrate for our expansion on foreign sales. He likes to represent *Spudnik* himself at International Trade Fairs and Farmer Expos. Greg doesn't speak a word of any foreign language, but he's the kind of chap who doesn't need to. He'll hug or shout or drink with strangers, and they'll get on.

I keep working at him. 'Look,' I said last year, 'there are already potatoes modified to absorb less fat when fried. You know what that means?'

He pondered for a moment. 'Crisper chips,' he decided.

'Bingo. Tell me that won't be popular. If we don't sell them, someone else will and take our market share. People *like* crisper chips.'

'We don't need it,' he said. 'We should concentrate on increasing the markets we have.'

Which at the latest count include Hungary, Spain, Portugal, the Canary Islands, Morocco, Algeria, Egypt, Israel, Oman, Saudi Arabia, Holland, Belgium, France and Ireland. A hard-won roster.

But regarding biotechnology: I accept Greg's qualms. Some say it's simply a development of traditional agricultural methods to improve healthy yields. Others, that it's fundamentally different, a hubristic tampering with nature's sovereignty. But this either/or dichotomy misses one simple point: that we all seem to think it just occurred yesterday to mad scientists, *Hey! Why don't we mess about with the genes of organisms? That'd be fun! Who knows what we'll find?*

When in fact, ever since Crick and Watson identified the double helix of DNA in 1953, research has continued, at an ever increasing pace, into the genetic make-up of plants and animals.

So what I've been trying to tell Greg is that what he and the public seem to regard as scientists' sudden presumption is in fact the opposite: they have been amassing and applying knowledge for fifty years, to the point where *not* modifying the genes they understand so well would be both absurd and a dereliction of their duty.

'Tell me about the loss of appetite,' the doctor said.

'It's ridiculous,' I said. 'I eat like a horse, I always have, just like my father. I love food. I mean I like good food, you know, I appreciate *haute cuisine* as well as anyone. But the act of eating. The experience of taking food into one's mouth, tasting, savouring texture as well as taste, biting and chewing it there, and swallowing. The mouth becomes, what? A cavernous realm of sensual pleasure.'

The doctor gazed at me. 'You've described it also,' he said, consulting his notes, 'as a hunger that eating doesn't satisfy.'

'That doesn't make a lot of sense,' I admitted.

'I don't disagree.'

'Those sound like two quite different symptoms.'

'One would have thought so.'

'When I do eat, I want to eat more. I can feel my stomach bloating, but still I want to consume. As if I want to fill every last space in my body, every last emptiness.'

'I'd like to have a look at your gut,' he said.

'What worries me,' I said, 'is that my father died of stomach cancer.'

'Ah. I see. Naturally, you fear that it may be hereditary.'

68

'Well, the incidence of cancer has been rising steadily for decades, hasn't it? But yes, it horrifies me. Cancer. The renegade cell.'

'That's how it begins. Remarkable, isn't it? An oncogene can differ from its healthy cellular counterpart by a single point mutation, the alteration of just one chemical rung in the double helix of its DNA.'

'Doesn't that worry you, Doctor?'

'Worry? It amazes me,' he said. He was a lot more excited by fatal disease than by good health, that was for sure. 'By the time a tumour has built up large enough to be detected, it'll already comprise a *billion* cells. All self-multiplied from that first oncogene.'

I shuddered. 'Unrestrained, anti-social growth,' I said. 'Destroying the body in which it grows. Insane.'

'Oh, you must bear in mind,' the doctor said, 'how stable our cellular system is. A large number of brakes and checks operate, you know: DNA repairs itself; cells die of their own accord after fifty doublings or so. I mean, it takes a lot for them to acquire cancer's unwanted immortality, and anyway, clumps of malignant cells soon stop growing unless they connect to the blood supply.' I began to reply but he cut me off: 'And what's more, our bodies have a mechanism for inducing aberrational cells to commit suicide.'

'Literally?'

'It's called apoptosis. Yes, really. Cancer demands a whole pattern of cellular behaviour that makes it unlikely to occur in a person's lifetime. But still, if it'd make you feel better, we'll take a look at your stomach.'

I began to stand up, pulling my shirt loose from my trousers. The doctor put up his hand.

'I meant from the inside,' he said.

I sat down, tucked the shirt back in. 'Is that going to be painful?' I asked. 'Will you use a general anaesthetic?'

'Local,' he said. 'I'll just pop a fibre-optic camera through your navel, and take a look.'

'Fine,' I said. 'You look where you need to. Wherever you want.'

'I'm not saying I'll find anything.'

I shook my head. 'I hope you don't.'

While I made to leave, the doctor seemed pensive. 'You know . . .' he said.

'What?'

'With your research . . .'

'Yes?'

'It's not bothering you?'

'No.'

'Just to say that, you know, genetic material is not dangerous. It's easily digested by gut enzymes.'

'I know that, Doctor,' I told him, and left.

I'M NOT sure what Greg would say if he knew about these consultations with my doctor. 'You hypochondriac wimp,' probably. I haven't mentioned them to him, nor to Lily. But I can be sure he'd like the technology. Why, he'd demand a diagnosis himself. Me, I'm squeamish, but Greg would love to lie back on a clinical couch with his belly button frozen with lignocaine and watch an overhead video of a camera tunnelling through his insides.

He's always been ahead of it all, has wanted gadgets to work more efficiently, faster. I remember when he bought his first car, other than our family firm vans. Automatic opening windows. They'd just come in then: you'd spot middle-aged men sat in their cars, waiting for their wives to come out of shops, pushing a button and watching the window slide down and up and down, like hypnotised children.

My brother? Within hours of getting his new saloon Greg was furious that the window didn't open quickly enough. If he needed the window opened then it had to be right NOW! He pushed the button and the window slid slowly, slyly down, and my brother gnashed and snarled at it. At least with the old kind of handle he could vent his impatience into wrenching the window open.

We had an argument the other day, Greg and I. I'd

suggested *Spudnik* sponsor a recipe book of microwaved potato dishes.

'Microwaves are shit,' he said. 'You've seen the research: it proves that microwaving spuds takes away aroma *and* flavour.'

'So?' I said. I told him he was the dim one, that the research was irrelevant. That microwave use won't stop increasing. 'Not enough people care about taste,' I told him. I pointed out that apartments are being built without kitchens: just a fridge, a kettle, and a microwave in the lounge.

'You Can't Beat 'Em,' Greg muttered as he marched out of my office. 'But You Can Fucking Microwave 'Em.'

What's the great thing about food? Fresh food? Its inbuilt obsolescence, that's what. Its blessed perishability. There are manufacturers of non-perishable goods I know who expend absurd amounts of energy attempting to justify the limited lifespan of, I don't know, their light bulbs, their automobiles. Dishwashers. CD players. The more sophisticated our engineering, the less durable become our goods. It takes phenomenally low prices to keep consumers from questioning this nonsense, but low they must remain, and shoddy the product, too, because turnover is essential. Right?

But for whom? For what? For profit? No. For growth. Turnover is essential. And I think of this short-termism, unnecessary for profit but necessary for the growth of the system itself, as individual companies' contribution to the greater good of the organic whole of capitalism. The moguls, after all, are fierce individualists behind their suits. Drakes and Raleighs. Buccaneers. They're mavericks who at the same time are captains of drone ships on the expanding ocean of capitalism on this enormous, this tiny, planet spinning in space.

\*       \*       \*

Until now we were shadows of each other. Grandparents. My father. My brother. Did I mention what Greg just bought for our mother? Mum enjoys a low-level hypochondria that I'm sure gets on everyone's nerves, and not just mine. She doesn't like to be without something to moan about.

'How are you, Mum?'

'I've got a bit of a throat, John,' she tells you. What a surprise. 'Liver's been playing up again, love.'

So Greg likes gadgets. Well, he just got Mum hooked up to medical telecare. He persuaded her private health clinic to get set up for bidirectional cable TV; there's a little camera stuck on top of her telly and a microphone beside it, and every day she has an online conference call with the nurse to check her blood pressure and heart-rate, and discuss any worries she has. She's been on this telecare for less than three weeks but already she's complaining less about her loneliness *and* her arthritis.

It was a stroke of genius to use television, since Mum watches it all day long. I don't have time for TV; the only time I ever see it is in the background when I visit my mother. Her favourite programmes are gameshows: she gawks at TV quizzes all afternoon. While her poor grandsons are groaning through tests at school, Mum – who surely hated exams herself just as much as they do – laps up puzzles, general knowledge, word-games on the goggle box. And what's so clever of them, these programme makers, is that they make sure their questions are so easy even my mother can answer them.

Anyway, credit where credit is due: my brother hits the spot sometimes. Though that's not all he hits. We've had video conferencing facilities in the company for a while, but recently a friend of Greg's was looking for someone to test his new prototype, so before we knew it *Spudnik* had upgraded from video to virtual conferencing with all necessary cameras installed in offices in each of our six centres: here and in Perthshire, Lincolnshire, Cambridgeshire, Herefordshire and Cornwall. So that meetings could be held with people – with their holo-grammatic counterparts – at any time. At the short-est notice.

At the moment we're making our first move into pro-cessing. We have a lot of growers in East Anglia, and we were wondering what market there was for the spuds that don't make the retail grade. And I said to Greg, 'Let's create our own.'

We're opening a potato processing plant in Cambridge-shire this May: the factory will process potatoes into dehy-drated flakes and flour for use in snack manufacturing. We plan at full capacity to convert over fifty thousand tonnes of raw spuds a year into eight thousand tonnes of finished product, for export to Europe; we've signed a contract with a major snack company. If this doesn't make money, nothing will.

'We're launching a snack attack!' Greg declared.

We're creating twenty-five, maybe thirty, new jobs. We want to hit the ground running and my brother's concerned about storage problems so, last week, he called the Packing Heads together. Clutching the last agronomy update and the latest crop report, Greg paced around our almost empty boardroom: the only other live entities were myself and our Marketing Director, but the rest of the seats were filled with ethereal figures. The ghostly heads of the Packing chiefs turning to follow my brother's impatience, his irritation.

'I don't see how we could have made things any clearer back in November,' Greg said. 'The climate's changing and our agronomists and our growers are adapting. Planting earlier. Harvesting later. Taking advantage. And you have to adapt, too, to different problems in storage. We had surface rots everywhere, and we diagnosed them as a mixture of blackleg soft rotting, blight, waterlogging. And pink rot.' He stopped, scanned the insubstantial faces. 'Vigilance was essential, we said. We told you.'

It was the warehouse manager in Lincolnshire who made the mistake of responding.

'We have been,' he said. 'Early warning of problems is essential. We know that better than anyone.'

'So what the hell is this?' Greg demanded, flourishing the papers in his hand. 'Fry colours variable. Overall quality indifferent. Increased levels of black dot and silver scurf.'

'That's right,' the Lincoln man said. 'That's what we told you.'

My brother was able to concentrate his attention on one ghost, while doing so in a grandstanding manner, for the benefit of the others. A natural bully's tactic, bringing spectators on to his side out of relief that it's not one of them he's picked on. 'Deterioration due to bacterial rots,' he continued, at the Lincoln man. 'Especially in Maris Piper, Bintje and Fianna, for Christ's sake.'

'Yes. Those varieties especially.'

'And what are we planning to use for this processing plant – *new* potatoes?'

My brother likes the holograms so much he believes in them. He's also aggressive in a provocative way that can make an opponent, if he possesses a similar confrontational nature, forget himself. The Lincoln warehouse manager was a tough ex-army bod, and he stood his ground.

'Don't read us the report like it's a riot act,' he said. 'We're the ones whose information made *up* the report.'

'Are you saying these rots are not there in store?'

'I'm saying of course they are. Who else would know better than us? I'm saying don't shoot the messenger.'

'I've had enough excuses!' Greg exclaimed. 'We put up with a lot of incompetence, but this is the last straw.'

Again he waved the papers, but this time in front of the flat nose of the warehouse man's virtual face. 'Foreign body contamination. If you cannot check that bulkers are clean and empty, and educate your staff to keep food and bottles and other crap away from the graders, then you are in the wrong sodding business, my friend.'

It was at this point that the warehouse man became as inflamed as my brother. He didn't like being called a friend. He stood up from his seat in an office in Boston, Greg stepped forward to meet him, and they came face to face. Each nose to nose with his hologrammatic opponent. Next thing we knew my brother took a swing at his adversary: he punched air, of course, lost his balance and fell over. Although I think I could have stopped myself, I burst out laughing – which gave everyone else permission to. Greg picked himself up, realised he'd look an even bigger fool if he sulked, and smiled at himself.

'All right,' Greg said, and tried to shake hands with the warehouse man – knowing he couldn't. He made a slapstick kind of a joke out of it, so then everyone was laughing with him, too, including his protagonist, and it was over.

If people think that's bad, it used to be worse when Greg drank. He quit ten years ago. Booze used to go straight to his voice: a couple of beers and he was yelling, and one thing invariably led to another. Who likes to be yelled at?

I was talking to my brother last week. He doesn't understand my thing for whores. 'You pay for it?' he asked. 'Aren't you worried?'

'Worried? Why? Of course I use rubbers.'

'I'd be on the lookout for bludgers. Ponces. You're an idiot.'

Then Greg hit me with another new fact about himself.

He's forty-seven years old and I thought I knew all about him. He said, 'I don't like to come.'

'Neither do I,' I said. 'Messy business.'

'I'm serious,' he said.

I laughed. 'Are you joking?'

'No,' he said. 'I prefer not to come. I like to hold it in.'

'Indeed,' I said. 'As long as possible. I'm sure you're a responsible and generous lover.' I'm sure he's not. Greg is the most impatient man I know. When talking, he gets so excited by the flow, the succession, of ideas in his head overtaking each other en route to his tongue that he interrupts himself. It's almost as if the person who's just spoken, who is in the midst of speaking, becomes a different, outdated self, suddenly superseded by this new person possessing a new thought; halfway through an irritating, obsolete sentence, the old self is to be interrupted and brushed aside. He must be an awful, impatient lover.

'When I ejaculate,' my brother said, 'I feel like I've lost something.'

'You mean,' I said, 'you don't like to come at all?'

'No.'

'Eventually, though. With her, right?'

'No.'

'But the bliss?'

'I feel like I'm losing part of myself.'

I didn't really know what to say. 'Do women like that?' I asked him.

'It takes them a bit of getting used to,' he admitted. 'Most women think they're failing me. I have to persuade them it's what I want.'

It's never too late to see someone in a new light. This is the era of communication, after all. In which an ever wider array of human beings all over the world come into nominal or potential contact with us – but with whom in reality we fail to communicate.

As Greg put it the other day at work, 'I cannot interface with these people!'

So we e-mail, nipping at each other's heels from screen to screen, our fax machines eat/excrete paper day and night, our digitalised voices leave messages across the counties and the oceans on voice mail, on answering machines. You phone a bureaucracy and spend whole hours on hold: music drones, interrupted only by occasional returns of a voice that assures you you're moving along in the queue, then the music resumes; whole songs, entire easy listening slabs of sound soothe your burning ear, your gritted teeth.

Greg claims that when BT realised there'd be a global telephone network with more connections than the human brain, they had a team of computer nerds trying to work out whether there was any danger of consciousness occurring.

Our IT guy at work told me the last time he came back to work from holiday, there were 417 messages on his computer. He suggested running a day course for our senior managers in multi-tasking: teaching them, including me and my brother, to type while talking on the phone; to check their pager, use their mobile and drive at the same time. 'We have to learn to cope with the data,' he said. He's right. People who want to make sure they get a message to me now seem to feel the need to send it in triplicate: by e-mail, fax and letter. Then they phone, just to make sure I got it.

I remember Lily stuck a notice on the door of our old place in town: NO FREE NEWSPAPERS, NO JUNK MAIL, NO RELIGIOUS CALLERS. But our name and address must have got on to some computerised database, and once that happens you're done for: this item of information spreads like a virus. My wife received new unasked-for catalogues for healthy living and environmental crusades every day; it drove her crazy, the trees cut down for this pulp. She printed self-adhesive labels saying, *Return To Sender*. But a lot of these companies are crafty, they don't put their address on the envelope.

There was one company, she kept sending back their catalogues, but every month a new one kept coming. So she got on to their website, and in the space for sending an e-mail she filled in her name and address and typed, STOP SENDING ME YOUR DAMNABLE CATALOGUE. She clicked on *send*, but an instruction came up on the screen telling her she hadn't filled in all the details. So she went back and saw she hadn't put her e-mail number in the allotted box. This she did, then clicked on *send* again, and the message duly travelled. And what happened? You guessed it: their company's catalogues did stop coming by snail mail, yes, but they started arriving by e-mail instead. Drives Lily mental.

Our nephews came over again the other day. There's a war going on inside Clint. What was divided between Greg and me, in our complementary temperaments, is crammed together between Clint's protruding ears. The introvert and extrovert, the reflective and the young man of action, the reader and the philistine; a contest prejudiced, I should say, by the need to appear a cool imbecile, and complicated by hormones, parental acrimony, the wealth of images telling him what to do, be, pretend.

It's no wonder Clint just sits there like a sullen, pimply oaf. I can hardly bear it sometimes. And then I get to thinking it'll be John Junior's turn in a dozen years.

The younger one, Lee, though, is still sweet, drifting along in his brother's wake. Actually, he's almost as tall as Clint now. He'd grown two inches in a week. He's making that sudden bolt into growth.

79

They both follow football. Like all boys. All citizens. Lee adorned in one of his team's many shirts, last season's away strip, this season's second reserve team kit. He lets himself be fleeced unblinking. Clint can take it or leave it, though not out of any cynicism. Rather, he appears not to care what people think of him. Is that possible? I may be wrong. Clint dresses scruffily but maybe that's his, or his mini-generation's, or his own grungy sub-tribe's, style. He *looks* as if whichever clothes his groping fingers discovered on the bedroom floor before he opened his eyes in the morning were dragged inside-out over his limbs. For all I know he might have spent an hour of careful selection, fine-tuning his bedraggled attire. He wouldn't tell me, would he?

Occasionally I attempt to wax nostalgic about footie with my nephews, I do my best to be pally with them, and describe the great players of my youth and twenties. Georgie Best and Jimmy Johnstone. The total football of Ajax, then Holland. Argentina's hysterical, pre-Malvinas, World Cup. The lost art of passing: Gerson, Netzer, Platini.

It doesn't work. When did it ever? I once dismissed my own father's foggy recollections of Johnny Haynes and Peter Doherty, but my nephews have added justification for their eyes glazing over, ears sealing off my droning tongue. 'You're talking pants again, Uncle John.'

For they have proof. Television betrays me. It doesn't matter what I tell them about, say, Don Revie's Leeds United, that mean but brilliant team who humiliated opponents yet ultimately stumbled, jittered, and failed to win the trophies they were ambling towards at the turn of the seventies. No, it doesn't matter what I say of Gray or Cooper's dribbling panache, of Giles' vision, of 'Sniffer' Clarke's nose for goal. Because the boys have seen enough games and highlights and goals transmitted. What should be the evidence that proves me right only proves me wrong. They have seen the men who in their prime look old already; unfit veterans, strollers, kicking the ball then stopping to rest when today's footballers run, run, run. These ghosts look more like park players than professional athletes. They look quaint, parodic.

The boys express an affection, however, which I didn't at first understand, for Denis Law.

'The King's great,' the younger one told me. He held the cuffs of his sixties special replica shirt tight to his palm with the nubs of his fingers. 'King Denis!' Lee exclaimed, commentator on himself, and he stuck his right arm up ramrod straight, and walked away, grinning.

Yesterday I came across them watching one of my old videos, and stood quietly behind them. I saw that it wasn't only the players who were unfit in those days. The cameramen were, too! Or the cameras were heavy, or the tripod hydraulics primitive. Whatever, the camera always seemed to get to Denis Law too late: his goals are all blurs. Someone in fuzzy black and white – Crerand, Aston – passes the ball, the camera swishes after it, one sees that something's happening but it's impossible to say what. Like an uncertain particle Denis Law disappears from view and no one can predict his direction or speed. By the time the camera's come to rest the ball is in the goal, the goalkeeper and one or two defenders are hauling themselves up from the mud, and Denis Law is walking away, grinning, with his right arm raised.

And what my nephews liked doing was rewinding, jogging the video back and forth on the Home Edit Suite, forwarding it in Xtreme Slo-Mo, and revealing for themselves what happened. Creating their own interactive TV; solving what Clint called the First Denis Law of Motion.

Yes, for this reason, at least, they rate him.

\* \* \*

I mentioned already that I saw our vocation as a holy one. It would be easy to drift in the opposite direction, to see one's customers, one's consumers, as animals. Like those magazine photos of someone standing beside the mountain of food they consume in a year. The thought of it all passing through them.

Greg and I did kid about diversifying into waste disposal. It was a running joke between the two of us for years. Drains. Water closets. Septic tanks.

'It's irresponsible to provide what's fed in one end,' Greg agreed, 'but neglect what craps out the other.'

We considered too the possibility of moving further, into the treatment of waste, the transformation of matter into manure, that could then be applied to the soil in which potatoes grew, and so complete a cycle. Gain control of the whole loop. A daydream alternative to growth, I hear people say? What do they know about economics? Better for them to keep quiet in the face of superior knowledge, I'd suggest. There is no alternative.

I was reminded of this speculative cycle recently, however, by a sardonic echo. We live in a village outside town, my wife and I and our baby son. In the Old Rectory, a crumbling Victorian pile we should never have shelled out for. No au pairs, no nanny, we do more ourselves than anyone I know, but we do employ a gardener. An enterprising young man in his late twenties, Richard, with a ponytail and trimmed beard and intelligent eyes, who in turn employs a raggle-taggle team of hired hands.

In the late autumn Richard's people came to us each week, and a couple of other gardens in the village, and did little other than bag up leaves. It was a major operation; a minor industrial process. There was one guy with a kind of hoover that blows instead of sucks leaves into swirling piles, a girl all padded up against the cold with a wide rake, another chap with wooden paddles with which he embraced huge armfuls of leaves that he then put into black bags. They bagged up the leaves and took them away.

This infuriated Lily. All last autumn, I'd come home on a Thursday and she'd tell me, 'Those gardeners put the dead leaves in plastic bags again!'

'It gives them work,' I'd say, and change the subject, because I didn't want to waste time talking about it. (I mourn the falling leaves only because in winter you can hear the drone, even in our village; the traffic drone all the way from the ring road, and the motorway.) I knew, somehow, what happened to the leaves: Richard's gang took the leaves away and added them to a huge pile of other clients' leaves on Richard's land. The leaves turned into compost. In the spring Richard's gardeners put the compost into green bags, and he sold the compost back to his clients. I don't know how I knew this; I didn't realise that Lily *didn't* know it. All she knew was that they took our leaves away somewhere, instead of making a compost heap in a corner of *our* garden.

Richard came to collect his money one Saturday and I overheard the conversation that ensued between him and my wife. Richard explained what happened to the leaves, just as I have. And I could tell, from the lilt in her voice, that Lily thought he was joking.

'Green bags. Of course. How much do you charge?' she asked, playing what she assumed was a respectable stooge in this comedy.

'Five pound a bag,' Richard said, and she laughed.

I assume his intelligent eyes helped prolong her misconception; he's got those eyes that tell you a person enjoys the absurdity of this life. Richard was also, on the other hand, a serious man.

'When they already paid you to take the leaves in the

first place. How many bags do you produce each spring?' my wife asked.

'Reckon about a thousand or two,' Richard said. 'It's top quality.'

'That's . . . how much?' she asked.

'Let's say it's a few thousand pounds,' he frowned.

'Oh, that's good. That's very good,' she said. 'You should do it.'

'We *do* do it.'

'No, really.'

'Yes, we've been doing it for years now.'

There was a long pause. When Lily spoke again, I could hear her voice was stretched like an elastic band. 'You should put our leaves on a compost heap in a corner of our garden,' she said.

'It's ugly,' Richard told her. 'Rich people don't want that in their garden. I'm sure your husband wouldn't want that.'

I smiled to myself. So I've made it, I thought, I'm rich. If our gardener says so, I must be.

'People's idea of what's ugly can change, though, as their understanding changes,' my wife argued. 'As the *idea* of a compost heap, of the process that's taking place inside it, becomes attractive, so the outside literally alters its appearance to us, and becomes more attractive, too.'

'No,' Richard said. 'I agree with you. You can say that, and I can say that. But rich people aren't like you and me.'

Now, either Richard somehow guessed that Lily was an aristocratic bohemian before she married me, and still felt herself ill at ease in the role of a merchant's wife, and he was bold enough to take her into his confidence in this way, despite the risk of offending me, her husband, or indeed herself; or else, owing precisely to the oddity of having this conversation at all, he overlooked the fact that she herself was one of his clients.

Anyway, the gambit worked. I heard, to my amusement, my wife say, 'You're probably right, Richard.' Her tone of voice suggested she even felt flattered by what he'd said. 'At least the leaves are being recycled. You deserve some reward for that.'

Recently, with this baby son with whom we've been blessed, my mind has once again been tuned to the digestive process, the flow of food. Which is just a little bit mind-boggling. Look at it this way: my wife, impregnated, ate and drank as usual, a little more maybe, and as well as food sustaining her there grew inside her a foetus, a baby. Her uterus expanded, pushing her bladder and intestines into corners of her torso.

John Junior fed via the umbilical cord but excreted in the normal way; yes, he peed and shat into the amniotic fluid in which he floated, which effluence was gradually broken down, filtered through and expelled from Lily's body.

After nine months my wife gave birth. And her body, as well as still taking what it needed for itself, stopped passing the goodness of what she ate on in the form of oxygen, salts, nutrients through her placenta and umbilicus, into a baby inside her womb, but rather transformed it into milk. To be suckled by the infant from her breast.

While our baby, for his part, as well as learning instantaneously at birth to fill his lungs with air and breathe, had to change the way he ate from a tube coming into his stomach to a nipple at his mouth, and milk down his throat. Which he accomplished impressively, I might add.

I've contemplated it, this process, as I've witnessed it these last weeks, and let me be honest, I still can't quite come to terms with it. The audacity, and ambition. How outrageous its inventiveness.

\* \* \*

'Did he say *John Junior*?' my wife beseeched our make-believe companion, when she overheard me call Jacob this. 'He called him *John Junior*? That is so laughably . . . *American*.' She turned to me. 'And so predictable.'

'And yet so apt,' I smiled.

Our son sleeps, utterly vulnerable. Wholly dependent upon us. Yet he is never so self-enclosed, so autonomous, locked in there in his dreaming mind.

Our baby sometimes sleeps with his mouth open. In the sunstream you can see all these motes of dust; I wonder whether there are microscopic animals there too. I think of my chubby son floating, a whale, his mouth open, the dust like krill.

# Wart Disease

Irregular shaped, warty galls
on shoots and eyes of young
tubers.
Do not confuse with severe
infections of powdery scab.

# MONDAY 11.30 A.M.

There's a filling station coming up.
I will explain to Greg and he will understand.

Insert the nozzle. Breathe those fumes. Why do men love the smell of petrol? I like to fill the tank, then squeeze more in to round up the price. Does everyone do that?

I'll tell Greg that ten million children a year die from infectious diseases that could be prevented with vaccines.

I drive around the ring road in a silent Merc. I forgot how much I enjoy driving. Greg updates our cars annually, I believe, and I just ask for the same model if it's available. So that it's as if I've had the same car for years but the engine just keeps getting quieter, the chassis smoother, the sound system cleaner every year.

These two natives who died, through no fault of mine or Simon's, did so for a noble cause. This is what I want to say. It may need reiterating.

Three years ago AlphaGen devised an experimental process for cholera, using bananas. They splice a strand of cholera DNA, via electrical pulses and simple bacterial cells, into the DNA of Agrobacterium, which naturally infects bananas. It's allowed to attack a banana cell, to which the cholera DNA is thus introduced. Hey presto: the banana cell begins to create proteins like those found in a cholera bacterium.

This banana cell is cloned and grown into a mature banana plant, whose fruit contains not cholera, quite, but rather cholera-copy proteins. When a person now eats such a banana their body responds as if it's been invaded by cholera bacteria: their immune system produces appropriate antibodies. Which will protect them against real cholera, should it come along.

Many things are getting faster, by the way, did I say that? Not just cars. My wife, for example, plays the piano. She's speeding up, I swear it. The well-tempered clavier? I hear Lily playing Bach at breakneck speed. The frenetic keyboard.

My wife and I met when I gave her a lift: she was hitching in a lay-by outside Stourbridge and I stopped the car. Lily reckons this is already a historical manner of meeting, since people don't hitch-hike any more, do they?

Now that we have a baby, we have a baby seat for the car. He's strapped in the back seat – and so is Lily, to sit beside our baby son. Yes, I can tilt the rear-view mirror and there she is, my pale English rose. Who when she's run down looks wan, listless, skinny. Nerves stretched, strung-out veins, too elongated for the heart that beats inside her. Etiolated. No rude red cells let into the bloodline for thoroughbred generations. Until me, I swam across the moat.

But that's not the whole story with Lily, oh no. Get her into an argument, or a dance class, bring a little colour to her cheeks, she can be vaulted to Olympian stature. With her cropped blonde hair, her imposing height, her lean athleticism. I do adore her. I want to squeeze her and hug her and hurt her.

And I would say, now I think about it, now that I'm deprived of the experience, that driving long journeys with

Lily sat next to me these past few years constituted one of the joys of my life. No, really.

Driving in the dark, talking. I wouldn't be surprised if it transpired that man had invented the motorcar for the purposes of conversation. And, yes, OK, as a place also in which to listen to music, drenching the interior of the vehicle with a wash of sound. That, too. Plus the funny thing is, it's dance music that sounds best in a cruising saloon, isn't it? I mean, you're not just sat down, you're strapped in, for God's sake! You can't move! You can't dance! Yet deep funk, rollicking Cajun, whatever – West African guitars, you name it. Hypnotic dervish trance, the seventeenth-century *Terpsichore* of Michael Praetorius, no less . . . they all sound magnificent through a good system in a smooth silent car. They sound like they were made to be played there.

What is it? Is it the movement of a car across the earth, the roll that with music becomes an otherworldly glide? Or is it a person's eye, the way that with a soundtrack the landscape you see is vitalised; the visual experience is aug-mented and becomes supra-cinematic? Or is it something else entirely, the fact that our lives have speeded up so much that only when hurtling through space at seventy miles per hour in this tin can are we able to relax sufficiently to actually stop still? And listen to music as music needs to be listened to?

But above all the car was invented as a chamber more conducive than any other place to intimate conversation.

What other joys? The letters Lily's written me when we've been apart. She used to travel. It was worth being apart for the pleasure of envelopes with exotic stamps and her scrawl; of other physical traces of her – scent, a smudge – on the paper inside; of her mind in words. Her affection for me expressed. She was all in the air then, a kite of a girl, I tied her down; I anchored her. I don't plan us to be apart again, and miss already those letters I expect to receive no more.

Happiness. And? John J. The way he loves to stand already; nineteen weeks old, even when he's bored, tired, fractious, help him to stand and he smiles, all pleased with himself. My son. His monumental little head.

And his birth. It's a story.

But driving with my wife. Those soul-baring, pain-sharing conversations in the dark that meander down into each other's deep waters. You can find the hidden shelves of misery, the fear of the black depths. Rising. Bubbles and light. Driving in the dark. And when we'd talked ourselves out, each drifting back into our own mind spaces as the car cruised along a motorway. Me steering the car. Lily's hand on my thigh. People would know what you mean. They've had that too. I miss it.

For no more. I am now alone up front, at the head, at the lonely prow of our vessel, sole navigator and pioneer. Lily's stuck in the back with our gurgling child. We are a family. We drive.

To tell the truth, it's a relief. Conversation with the same person gets exhausting, doesn't it? Marriages talk themselves out, just run out of gas. There's that awful moment, isn't there, when you think, this is so great, we can sit here in utter contentment without having to even say anything. Because you realise immediately, oh my God, we've nothing left to say to each other. This nothing balloons in front of you and between you, and for ever for the rest of your hemmed-in lives.

But what can you do? Can you keep something back in reserve? Of course not. You can't stop talking. Except that yes, actually, you can. You can have a kid.

*  *  *

Lily and I celebrated our fifth wedding anniversary this year. We got married in the Register Office with just Greg and Lily's friend Mira as witnesses, then we had a ritual devised by Lily in a barn on her parents' property. Jesus, what a mish-mash it was! A Sufi love poem, something by Donne, the Beatitudes and platitudes from Kahlil Gibran. We were prayed for by this woman priest and blessed by that Hare Krishna monk. Music provided by bohemian pals of Lily's. A circus. I let her have whatever she wanted. I mean, I put up a good deal of resistance, of course. How can a woman enjoy what she's won if she hasn't had to fight for it? You have to know when to give way. What do I care what kind of wedding we had?

Lily was a traveller. A hippy. The Near, the Middle, the Far East. She spent winters in Goa, Bali, an island in the Gulf of Thailand, came home for spring laden with jewellery and trinkets she sold to shops here and there. The first years of our relationship Lily stayed with me through the summer and took off again in the late autumn. I decided she was mine for keeps early on, but it took Lily longer to accept it. This man, this reserved, ambitious businessman, pulling her down, pegging her back. At the same time, her body was settling, and the urge to bear children grew stronger: bearing children made more and more sense to her, as the thing to do with her body. She'd seen enough middle-aged women still out there on the road, lined, brown, hollowing out. They disgusted her, she once told me. Frightened her. Lily knew she couldn't carry on the feckless life.

We spent years trying to have a child.

As it became clear that this wasn't happening of its own sweet accord, Lily turned methodical. She worked out the precise breakdown of her cycle, bushwhacked me around the flat. Clutching a stop-watch, she'd demand ejaculation.

You oblige over-eagerly at first. Till you realise this is what it's like making love with a religious fundamentalist. It's no fun; you soar off into reluctant reveries. But that was just the start of it. We'd been married two years when Lily got pregnant, only to lose it after a few weeks, and this miscarriage made her more determined than ever: for the next year or so I enjoyed conjugal relations with a mad scientist.

We had tests. We gave samples of everything we could, and it turned out they reckoned it was me. I had weak motile velocity. Low sperm count. Insipid fertility. They tried various treatments. One time they incubated some of my sperm inside a dead mouse until it could be used in IVF treatment. A vain palaver that was. It is odd, though: I'm quite sure if Lily knew what we'd go through and how far we'd go, she'd never have got us started.

She cooks me potatoes, Lily, she knows I appreciate it. There's an Italian soufflé she makes of potato mashed with butter, milk, eggs and parmesan, with another whole bunch of mozzarella and fontina put in the middle. She bakes it in the oven until it's got a crispy brown crust, and serves it with a rocket salad and this pesto made from grinding parsley, toasted almonds and olive oil, with parmesan stirred in. Last time she doled it out the nephews were here. I said, 'Don't waste this on them, Lily. Give these tykes a burger or something.' But they're not as stupid as they look. They enjoyed it too.

I once told Lily how the poorest Irish used to keep a thumbnail long, for peeling their boiled potatoes as they ate them. Now, if Lily spots a guitar player, with fingernails on one hand kept long, she'll nudge me and whisper, 'Must be an Irish musician.'

In the nineteenth century people dug their spuds up from

94

their allotments in October and stored them by clamping: piling them on a raised piece of ground and covering them with straw and soil, with vertical stalks of straw for ventilation.

I told Lily about that and she tried clamping some potatoes in her vegetable garden: she reckoned it didn't store them too well. She keeps Richard and his crew out of her organic plot, where she grows beetroot, carrots, onions, leeks, cabbage, artichokes, and herbs and so on. Me, I keep out of it, too. I see her bent over the soil.

'It'll be bad for your long back, darling,' I tell her. Lily doesn't appreciate how odd I find the whole business: I just can't shed the idea that fruit and veg should come into the kitchen straight from a warehouse in the yard.

Lily wouldn't allow Richard to use *Round-up* around the trees he planted beyond the orchard; the poor chap had to hack at the tough grass there and put mulch mats down. I tell her she reminds me of the Victorian horticulturalists. There was one fellow called James Clark, who worked from his home and his greenhouses in Christchurch, Hampshire. Clark had a commercial relationship with the Sutton seed family, who bought and marketed his many successful varieties of potato – one of which, Epicure, is still grown today, amazing when the average life of a variety then was still less than twenty years. Another was his Magnum Bonum of 1876, a white, kidney-shaped late maincrop, with a floury texture and blandly sweet flavour, that became this country's biggest-selling potato and remained so for the rest of the nineteenth century. It grew vigorously, withstood blight and yielded well year after year, until towards the end of the century it became susceptible to virus infection and seed stock degeneration, and finally dwindled.

We were talking last week. 'Salmonella. BSE,' Lily was

saying, shaking her head. 'Foot and mouth. Two a penny imports.'

'The British livestock industry's on its knees,' I said. 'If our *arable* farmers are hobbled in the race for new high-yielding crops, you can wave goodbye to agriculture in this country.'

'So accelerate organic conversion,' she said.

'The highest-yielding organic potato in the latest national trials was one *Spudnik* developed with our Scottish boffs,' I protested. 'But we're talking about what is all and ever will be a small niche in the market.'

'Why?'

'Why? Because most people want cheap food. They don't give a damn what's in it or where it comes from. You told me yourself.'

'What did I tell you?'

'That people on this planet are the dregs who refuse to become enlightened. The signs are all around saying, *this is all you have to do*, but they resolutely ignore them.'

'What? That is so totally different, John.'

'Anyway, organic farming can't feed everyone, that's why.'

'Then there are too many people,' my wife said.

How can you argue with that? I mean, what can you say? All you can say is, yes, you're right, darling. Of course there are too many people on this little island. On this little planet. There were three billion in 1960. Six billion now. Before our son's fifty years old he'll be surrounded by twelve billion unique individuals.

'Oh, wake up, man,' Lily said, as she does whenever she considers me obtuse. Usually embellished: 'Wake up, why don't you?' It's a line of hers that ends up just where it came from, an ambiguous spot midway between a partner's private joke and spousal putdown.

\*      \*      \*

96

What I've come to realise is that Lily's vehemence is insubstantial. It's all display. She buzzes around you but actually there's no sting. Her parents both died within a year of our marrying. Pure coincidence. They, especially her father, whom Lily adored, had that languid arrogance of the upper classes. What they had hardly any left of was the money. It's the money that allows these people to get away with their charm. When I was introduced to them her father poured drinks and we stood, more side by side than face to face, G and Ts in hand. He bore an eye-patch.

Papa chinked the ice in his glass and said to me, 'Food, isn't it?'

'Isn't what, sir?' I said.

'The, er, your, er . . . Family business, eh?'

'Potatoes, sir,' I said. 'Spuds. We grow them, we buy them, we sell them.'

With each verb he winced, then smiled weakly.

By the time the inheritance reached Lily there wasn't any; the poor girl was penniless. But the assumption that the menial needs of life would be taken care of had been bred into her. So that she starts off telling me how things are with this vehement self-belief, until it's as if some trigger in her brain is pulled, the reminder that actually she has no money, she has no power. The trigger I only have to wait for. For then, almost without being aware of it, Lily simply retreats. Shuts up. Steps aside.

Our baby son is fat and healthy and it's hard to resist smooching him. Don't get me wrong. I don't resist; I indulge myself. Me and my boy canoodle. 'I'm putty in John Junior's hands,' I told my wife the other morning. ''Cos he's a putti in my hands.' A weak pun, but with a cultural allusion, at least, that I assumed Lily might appreciate.

'Jacob,' she said. 'And it's plural.'

'What?'

She turned away, mumbling, 'Nothing.'

'No, what?' I said. 'Come on. What's plural?'

I guessed she had corrected me – and was now retreating from so doing. She couldn't help herself, the over-educated bitch. In that case, I couldn't help myself either.

'I said, what's plural?'

'It's not important.'

'Tell me.'

'Darling, just that "putti" is plural. The singular is "putto", actually. That's all.'

First thing in the morning I lie with my son beside me and make notes, calculations, plans. My brain functions well before dawn, with a first cup of tea. I'll be on the bed in the spare room having brought John Junior there after his last feed, at 5 a.m., so that his mum can get some undisturbed sleep. Undisturbed by my snoring, his snuffling and squeaking, her restless men.

John Junior moves in his sleep: the first substantial ambulation of my son's life. He does a sly shuffle off his sheepskin, a turn over on the mattress, until you realise that he's reached you. I mean, you set him down a foot or two away and suddenly he's up against you. And why not? He's friendly. He likes people. He appreciates the reassurance of a human being's pulse, the touch of our skin, our body heat.

How did I say I met my wife? Hitch-hiking? Surely not. I don't pick up scroungers, I've never been that desperate for company. No, we met playing football, Lily and I.

I might have said before that I used to play, half a lifetime ago, for a team in a local league. My only hobby. A mediocre full-back, that was me. A clean and decent tackler, willing to take the ball off the keeper and play it out from the back. Defence as the first line of attack, and all that. I loved the game, the combination of physical and mental, destructive and creative in the same unfolding moment. I appreciated the comradeship, too. I rarely went boozing with the lads afterwards, I don't mean that beery camaraderie. I was usually straight back to work. But the intense fellowship on the pitch.

Being a father's like being a footballer again: always carrying some niggling injury. Lifting and bearing a small baby in awkward postures. Then, the twanged muscles were in your legs – now they're in your back or shoulders. Anyway, I quit in my early thirties. Which is to say the game quit me, it spat me out. When you turn all of a sudden slow and cumbersome, this activity you loved becomes embarrassing. You cannot justify it. Kids go galloping past you. You foul them out of spite. The manager selects you on sentiment. The very ball changes its nature; this once-friendly sphere becomes volatile, difficult to anticipate; before you know it, it's beyond you. You are in the process of being discarded. So you retire.

That's the end of real football, but it needn't be the end of everything. You can join a veterans' team, you can coach kids, you can play five-a-side in the Council Sports Hall with florid-faced overweight mates on a Wednesday night. Or you can join in a kind of community kick-around that took place on a Sunday morning on the local rec, a couple of hundred yards from where I used to live, off Beardsley Lane. Who started it I don't know, and there didn't seem to be an organiser. But around ten, ten-fifteen on a Sunday morning, a motley assortment of individuals would congregate on that marshy green patch by the canal, just past the playpark. There were men and women and kids. I seem to remember now that it was my nephew took me, yes, I was looking after little Clint for the weekend and I yanked a carrier bag containing mouldy boots and shinpads out of the cupboard under the stairs and went along with him and one of his little buddies.

There were twenty-odd people altogether, of the widest array of age and ability imaginable, and I played indulgently. I wanted anyone who knew about football to see that here was a once-fit and talented player nobly fulfilling familial obligations. No sliding tackles, no swerves around children, no easy headers for me. I let mothers dribble past me, I passed the ball to the smallest child on my team. I took a couple of gentle pots at the opposition goal, shots so devilishly flighted that they invited spectacular saves from a pint-sized keeper, diving to push the ball around the pile of clobber standing in for goalposts.

I'll admit the truth right now: I went back to that rec kick-around almost every Sunday for the next couple of years. Why? Because I haven't ever enjoyed football more than I did there. I'm not saying it was better than the real thing, no, but it was just as good, in its peculiar way. And it was football. It was as if what I loved about the game, putting thought into action in this physical activity, was still at the heart of the experience, but it was now of an intriguingly different nature. Instead of creating with and struggling against more or less equal athletes, one had an additional set of calculations brought into the equations being made in one's head, through the vastly differing ability of each participant. Instead of going for a loose ball at the same time as an opponent and thinking only, 'I'm going to get there first,' you had to weigh up the sex, size, speed of the approaching figure, as well as assess what kind of game they were having, what a boost to his or her confidence it might be for a fat, slow eight-year-old child to nick the ball off me.

My future wife turned up, she must have come with someone. I was thirty-five, Lily was ten years younger. A lean blonde in shiny leggings. She got picked for the other team from me, immediately placed herself in the centre-forward position, and proceeded to take no interest or part in the game until the ball came rolling towards our goal, whereupon Miss Twinkletoes came to life, revealing quick feet and thought, and tried to boot it in. She was nimble, with a woman's low centre of gravity, able to change position, to readjust the alignment of her body in response to bobbles and deflections. In short, she scored goals. She enjoyed herself, and kept coming back, improving each week. As for me, I continued to manoeuvre myself on to the opposing team, and I man-marked her, ever tighter. I also spoke to Lily on and off through the game.

'You're too slow. You've put on weight since last week.'

'Leave me alone,' she said, but I stalked her around the pitch. I marked her so tight no one could see I was holding her cycling shirt, or whispering in a crowded area, 'I know what you're going to do. You're too predictable.'

'Piss *off*,' she said, trying to elbow me away, but it only took Lily a couple of weeks to get a dialogue going. I let her outpace me, kicking the ball and rushing after it from the halfway line towards a small boy taking his turn in goal, with me flailing behind, easing off the pedal so as not to catch her, until from three yards she thumped the ball home.

'Who's slow now?' Lily crowed in my face as she jogged back past me.

Or I made to take the ball off her with legs bowed so that she couldn't help nutmegging me, shrieking, 'See you around, fatface.'

It wasn't always easy. Other times I nicked the ball off Lily's foot as she was about to score an open goal. As our combat developed, I shoulder-charged her adroitly, knocking her off balance and over; not enough to hurt her, I don't mean, just enough to bring her blood up. To let her know I was there. Hey, she could dish it out herself:

I'd run off with the ball, chuckling, and she'd chase me. Kick my ankles as hard as she could. But yes, I bundled Lily into puddles, mistimed tackles so ineptly that I took her by mistake instead of the ball and we slalomed across sloshy grass. We performed, it seemed to me, a muddy and delicate tango of courtship one late, wet English spring. When the ball was out of play we needled each other, until I felt bold enough to ask her for a drink afterwards.

That was that. We got together, and Lily promptly announced her withdrawal from the beautiful game.

'I thought you were never going to say anything,' she said. 'I'd just about given up.'

'I thought you enjoyed it,' I said.

'I was beginning to,' she admitted. 'But let's face it, football's cold and wet and muddy and dangerous. I mean, wake up, man. It's a pointless activity.'

Lily fell in love with me. Not immediately, no, not at first sight. Hardly. Rather, over a short period of time after the first time we made love. I wish I could explain it but I can't. It's not the kind of thing you ask someone, even when they're your one and only.

'Tell me, Lily, how did it happen? How did your feelings for me develop, exactly?'

You can't do it. So I don't know. It was a mystery. A miracle that I understood was taking place with each date we went on, each conversation. This beautiful woman invaded my solitude. She stared into my eyes, and dazzled herself. This amazing stranger was asking me to kidnap her. She was falling in love.

Ten years together, five years married. That's an achievement.

I wonder whether John Junior will play football. I hope he grabs the joy from it that I have. Improvising patterns with the movement of one's own and other hurtling bodies *and* sliding in the mud. I suspect that the only people who really appreciate this earth are footballers and gardeners. And potato growers, obviously. The alluvial land around the River Severn, grade one, or over in the Fens where you can find thirty feet of topsoil full of nutrients and not a stone to be struck. Or grade-two land in Herefordshire, where with the import of cheap fruit in the seventies and eighties farmers ripped their orchards out. That was when we came in; just as we'd done in Cornwall after the wholesale markets there shrank to nothing, and offered farmers a lifeline.

When Lily and I met we fell mutually in unrealistic love; we didn't know each other at all. She smuggled the smells of the world into my flat in a town in the English Midlands, threw them into the air in the kitchen. Lily already had the ability to conjure up meals for half a dozen friends out of a quick trip to the market. She'd stagger up the steps of my flat like a rucksacked mountaineer in training, lugging her own weight in veg, and haul it into the kitchen, there to reenact a battle scene at the cooker and a naval disaster in the sink. From this mayhem there'd appear upon the dining-room table the most delicious four-, five-course meals, served by a ladyship so serene she gave the impression they must have been prepared below stairs by an army of hirelings. With flowers, candles, napkins improvised from loo paper, with designs felt-tipped fresh upon them. Our guests were spoiled.

The next morning I'd creep early from bed and before leaving for work soak burned pans with crystal soda, scrape cutlery, wipe plates and bowls, dry up, scour the cooker and mop the floor. And while I was washing up I marvelled at this woman of the world and why she'd deigned to share herself with me. Her protean creativity, her generous energy, her competence: enchanting. What she'd done was utterly beyond me. Me and cooking don't mix. My main problem is I panic.

Everything about Lily delighted me. I reckoned I could spend my whole life watching her move, speak, stand still. Lovemaking would always be this good, this unhurried frenzy. But then you wake up one day and life has done a backward flip: the endearing intimacies you shared have become hideous.

'Another thing,' she said towards the end. 'At night when you piss.'

'I try not to wake you,' I interrupted. 'I tiptoe to the bathroom. I sit down.'

'You always wake me,' she said. 'And when you piss at night, you fart. Always.'

I thought about it. It was true. 'You can hear that?'

'How can I not hear it? I mean, is it something about sleep, about lying down, that means gas collects in your rectum?'

I shrugged. It seemed possible she was bluffing, having heard it once one sleepless night.

'It's disgusting,' she winced. 'I wait for it. I can't help myself. I wait for that little . . . exclamation.' She shook her head, as if at the sheer unfathomability of the fact that she'd wound up with me.

As for the alchemical meals Lily produced, I began to tire of getting up early the next morning to tidy up. But she hated me to wash up before guests had left, when I did so once or twice she gave me the hardest time, so I'd do it after she'd gone to bed. I'd stand there at the sink dead-eyed with drink and sodden fatigue, thinking of work the next day and cursing the woman for creating Armageddon in our kitchen every time one of her friends dropped by, when who had to clear it up? She threw a meal together and I picked up the pieces after midnight.

Did I say end? That was the end of the beginning. Every couple has to go through that, I suppose. You've got to work through it if you're going to stay together.

Lily is an extremely competent woman. Travellers tend to be. I'm always telling her, 'Darling, you can cook in eleven languages. This is delicious.'

She does the nicest thing: she cooks us potatoes in ways they're prepared around the world. It's a present she gives me. The other Saturday, Melody and her husband, Bill, dropped by; they were there when I got back from tennis. Lily invited them to stay for lunch, I gave Melody a Vermouth, poured Bill a pint of beer. He wears polo-shirts, tucked into his belt: they stretch, ever tighter, over his paunch. I ply the fat oaf with beer any chance I get, just to help him get even fatter, which is really stupid because what I can't stand is the idea of him spreading himself over my sister.

You'd think Melody might drift through to the kitchen, to chat with Lily, but the fact is they're wary of each other, my wife and my sibling. They've each confided, 'John, I don't think Melody/Lily likes me.' Which is absurd. What do they think, these women? That they're in competition?

Lily was gone a few minutes, then called us through for potato peanut soup. 'I discovered this in Ghana,' she revealed. She garnished the soup with spring onion, unsalted peanuts, and thin strips of deep-fried plantain. It was creamy from the puréed potatoes, hot from crushed red chillies, and nutty.

Melody tasted with her eyes closed and said, 'There's ginger, isn't there? There's ginger.'

Perhaps there was no catastrophe awaiting Melody in adulthood, but one thing has always diminished her: the reflection of her childhood. For no kind of life could fulfil the promise of the golden child, the favoured one.

For Melody, the rare beauty of her age in our community, heroic status was necessary. A Helen, an Atalanta. How this could translate into modern life, I suppose, would have been through fame as a model, a singer, a dancer.

I suspect it's almost impossible for us to believe that beautiful people cannot see themselves. Many women may, it's true, build up through reflections in mirrors and other people's behaviour a perpetual self-image. But Melody's simplicity militated against her acquiring this extra sense. When in adolescence she did realise how people looked at her, with wonder and hunger and envy in their eyes, it provoked less a willingness to see herself as others saw her than a wary retreat from any centre of attention.

So that it's impossible to say whether the way Melody's life developed was as disappointing to her as it was to those who know her. Hers has been an ordinary life. In her early twenties she married a colleague in the Town Planning department, where she worked as a secretary. Bill Sutcliffe. A man who has risen tenaciously through the cut-throat world of council bureaucracy to become Assistant Chief Inspector of Works. A responsible citizen, a good father to their three children, a dutiful husband. Who, far from being grateful every day for his good fortune, gives the impression that he's as oblivious to Melody's beauty as she is herself. He takes my sister for granted, and she does not object.

'PEOPLE CALL it Sudden Adult Death Syndrome,' the doctor told me.

'This is precisely what I'm worried about,' I said.

'Actually, it's not a syndrome at all. Merely a phrase with which to categorise a whole bunch of unexplained deaths.'

'Right. Which is exactly what worries me.'

'One moment someone's fit and well, the next they're dead. Two hundred people a year, that's what we're talking about. In a population of sixty-five million? Please. You may as well fret about spontaneous combustion.' The doctor chuckled. 'Or being hit by a falling block of ice. If you want something to fear, why not make it more dramatic, at least?'

'All right. You've made your point,' I nodded. 'Very humorous. But what's the likeliest cause, do you think?'

With a frown and a sigh, the doctor gave a shrug that said, as politely as he could in his position, Who cares? 'Some kind of heart-rhythm disturbance. Probably.'

'You see?' I said. 'It does happen.'

'We all of us have moments of arrhythmia. The heart rights itself immediately. It's harmless, believe me. And other possible causes have been put forward. Epilepsy, if I remember right. Undetected brain defects. No pattern has been identified, you see. If you don't mind me saying so, paranoid hypochondria doesn't suit you. It doesn't fit your health consumer profile.'

'I agree,' I said. 'I was just thinking, that's all.'

'Now, tell me about this ache,' the doctor said.

'The ache in my bollocks.'

'Oh. You didn't mention where it was.'

'I didn't? It's an occasional mild throb.'

'Where?'

'If I try to locate it exactly, if that's what you'd like me to do, I'd say that if I have two balls, one floating more or less above the other in my scrotal sac, the ache emanates from one of them. The lower one.'

'A dull ache, you say?'

'A mild throb, yes. Unpleasant, but only, I think, because of where it is. We're nowhere more vulnerable, Doctor, than there, wouldn't you say? What do footballers protect? The eyes? The brain? No.'

He examined me. His analytical, lifeless medic's fingers felt my scrotum, fingers that prejudged nothing. Fingers somehow exasperatingly non-committal. Fingers that refused to discover and squeeze an unfamiliar shape with trembling excitement, as if to say, 'Got it! Found it! Here it is!' And, by implication, 'We can cure it!'

No. Not at all. He just held my testes in his dull hand as if weighing them; thoughtful, disengaged.

A MAN alone drives his car, around the ring road. As each sign and roundabout becomes familiar, recognition scores a groove. However satisfying this is, though, it can't be right. Because a vehicle is made for progress. Transportation from here to there, this place to that. The point of a car is its forward movement; it wasn't designed for prevarication.

Soon, then, I shall turn off, divert myself, to work.

The other day we had some of Lily's friends round. Before dinner, of a dozen vegetable curry dishes, Lily had made a snack of small rotis: potatoes mashed with chillies, cumin, turmeric, fresh coriander, rolled in flour and fried. Served with a coconut and mint chutney. I brought a bottle of vodka from the freezer and poured some clean cold shots.

'A man could live on your starters, Lily,' one of our guests said.

'Hey, that's my line,' I told him. This chap, Jerry, was a painter. Later, during the meal, they were talking about art, and Jerry set off on a long riff about the consequences for painting of mechanical reproduction i.e. of photography. Its realism had not only mocked and ruined figurative painting, as we all knew, but the mechanical speed of which it was a part, hurrying people ever faster through the twentieth century, had made it finally unbearable for western citizens to sit still, posing for a painting, for the hours necessary to do a decent job.

'People are twitchy,' he said. 'Not just in their minds, either; in their very muscles.'

'You're right,' Lily said. 'A hundred years ago everyone had the patience to pose for a painting.'

So what was a modern figurative painter to do? Jerry asked us. Why, use photographs, of course. 'Most women can be persuaded to strip and parade themselves for half an hour: long enough to shoot a roll or two of film. Photography they understand,' he said, 'they accept the glamorous voyeurism of the photographer half-hidden behind his camera. But the painter's frank, open gaze? No, sir, by *that* they feel threatened, offended, abused.'

And so the poor painter with his palette of colours built up over millennia is left alone in his studio with a clutch of sweaty photographs, pathetic chemical reproductions from which to infer the subtle musculature, the texture of flesh. The infinitely variable pallor of skin. The shifting concavities and convexities of a human body.

Jerry shook his handsome head. 'Technology's ultimate, sardonic triumph over art,' he moaned.

I didn't say anything. Poor sap. People who bemoan the speed and direction of the traffic get caught up in it eventually, and choke on other people's fumes. Or else they sit it out at the side of the road, going nowhere. The only place to be is out front, isn't it?

The nephews dawdled over yesterday. I was outside, conversing with the men installing our security system, when they came loping down the drive. Gangling, awkward strangers. Clint, I swear, walks with a scowl. Like those rappers he admires on MTV. Each generation comes up with new ways of walking.

Teenagers are like babies, with the same sudden speed of brain growth. It's why they look grotesque to those who love them: their physiognomies are literally being forced into new shapes.

It was lovely outside, so Clint drew the curtains and the boys holed themselves up in a gloomy corner of our sitting room, watching TV and playing the mini-discs they bring with them. Lee, when he is allowed by his brother in their ruthless sibling jungle to put on his discs, still likes music with traces of melody in it. Some of this hip-hop stuff is listenable, inventive even, to my duff old ears. But there's one kind of techno Clint plays, gabber he calls it, that, when one is unwittingly besieged by it, is the aural equivalent of being hit. It's the opposite of background music, it's foreground music, it's a wall in front of you. The listener is removed behind it, steps into the background himself. It makes Lily march into the room and yell, 'Please turn that noise off!' And he does. It gives her a sore head. It gives everyone a headache, including Clint, though smoking and drinking and sniffing glue give a person a headache and he doubtless does those, too. Maybe that's what being a teenager is all about: learning to cope with different ways of giving yourself a sore head.

Clint's a pain but last week he deigned to explain that it wasn't his fault, he was obliged to develop an attitude. It was essential for survival on the streets, he said. 'You gotta look right,' Clint told us in his gravelly voice. 'Or they rag you. I can't be messing with that.'

Attitude. A vacuous and admirable quality. I imagined it was more than youthfulness, this, that we are inside an era in which virtues and vices have exchanged and mutated. Naivety is a vice. Being a poor dancer another. Failure to decipher on first hearing the garbled lyrics of popular song.

*      *      *

While the boys stayed in our house yesterday Lily and I took the baby for a walk, a stroll around the village. We are settling in. We'd been living here for about five minutes when some old biddy knocked on the door and asked whether we'd like to offer the use of our lawn for the summer fête, as the previous occupants had, and would my wife, furthermore, consent to *open* the fête? Lily spent the next few days sniffing and snooting at the class-ridden traditions of English social life by which villages, this village in particular, were still clearly strangled, and how mad we were to have moved here. It was the background she'd managed to escape and she resented me, the *nouveau riche* who'd seduced her, dragging her back into it. But I could tell that in some way she didn't want to acknowledge she was tickled pink, and that summer – last year – with eventual good grace my wife, visibly, elegantly pregnant in a specially purchased Donna Karan grey cotton trouser suit, made a short speech and cut a ribbon and declared the church fête open.

We'd first visited the village together when we came to one of the concerts they have in the church here. Lily's the musician. She plays the piano. Me, I like music in films. The Mozart in *Amadeus*. *Chariots of Fire*. That's where I appreciate music.

The choirmaster in this village church, it turns out, is an enthusiast who four times a year – on the Saturdays before Palm Sunday, Whit Sunday, All Saints' Day and Advent Sunday, according to the programme – persuades musicians of international renown to play. For free. The Allegri Quartet it was that first time we went. Since then, such as Nigel Kennedy, Evelyn Glennie. All proceeds to casting a new bell or digging a well in Africa. The medium-sized Norman church gets packed, sold out months in advance, and the atmosphere is really quite odd. The whispering acoustic that churches possess may not be perfect for classical music but it makes for, you know – yes, I'll say it: a holy ambience. Why not? Let all churches become concert halls, that's what I say. Non-denominational musical chambers. Jazz joints, heavy-metal dives. Nightclubs, cabarets. Clear the pews and let the organ's pomp fill the nave! For pensioners' tea dances! Rock 'n' roll hippodromes, world music jamborees. Techno discothèques for our doomed and deafened youth.

Let there be epiphanies we can all own up to. Because, of course, if we're honest, these four concerts a year in our village church are stymied by a polite, a pious holding back in the manner and the attention of the congregation. That is to say, I mean: the audience. The memory of worship in the place needs to be exorcised once and for all. The religion needs to be cleanly transcended.

Anyway, during the interval on that very first visit we joined a procession to a big house in the village for refreshments, and Lily and I found ourselves whispering to each other, 'I'll take that house.' A Regency mansion here, an Edwardian farmhouse there. 'You can have that one.' Even the brick-built bus shelter looked like it was probably a listed building. The council estate where the skivvies lived was tucked neatly out of the way. We spotted a *For Sale* sign posted outside the Old Rectory, and Lily said, 'Sweetheart. We could share this one.'

I said, 'Be serious. Do you want me to tell you how much they'll be asking for it?'

But the next day Lily got details from the estate agent and the house was a lot cheaper than I'd told her it would be. I'd snared myself. It was *in need of modernisation* i.e. it was falling apart. It is beautiful, though, isn't it? People see this place, they think, that guy has made it big time! Ah, I should never have let Lily persuade me. We were already investing all our money in our child. I had to swallow my pride and go beg a bigger mortgage. And don't talk to me about repairs!

The fact that there's a primary school, led by an energetic young Head, with pre-school activities like a music group and an infants' gym, still thriving in the village, convinced us, planning a family as we were. Yes, we talk about education already. At cross-purposes, on the whole. The other day I gave Lily my opinion that by the time our son starts school, teachers will be redundant, replaced by software designers. Kids will learn everything on computers.

'We'll still go to PTA meetings,' I said, enjoying myself. 'It'll be the Parent Technician Association.'

'That is so typical of you people,' Lily said. 'You don't want to educate children, you want to programme them.'

'No, listen,' I said, but she didn't.

'Just because you overcame a dismal early education, you think no one else needs one,' she said, knowing that Greg and I, meritocrats both, vowed long ago that we'd send our children into public education, not just primary but secondary level too. Though the truth is that my brother's children are the result; his boys have set an example I don't intend mine to follow. It's a vow I'll gladly renege upon when the time comes. Ever wonder why evolution is such a slow process? You only have to stand outside Clint and Lee's school gates at half past three one afternoon: it's because the ugly reproduce themselves at a terrifying pace. Retarding the species. The beautiful are content to swan around looking lovely when they should be buckling down to it, procreating with purpose.

'You know, darling, you may be right,' I told Lily. 'Maybe he *should* have a classical education. The best schools we can afford. Latin and Greek. Rhetoric, debate. Uniforms and manners and punishment. Rough games.'

I know this is far from what Lily has in mind. She envisions liberal, progressive – if equally expensive – regimes. She throws names at me: Piaget, Steiner, Montessori. I feign the ignoramus.

'I don't deny that public schools teach boys to think,' she said. 'Look at them all, heads cut off from their bodies. They can't do anything *but* think. Wake up, man. They're even worse than that drug-dealing den Jacob's cousins attend.'

At times like this I give up. Nod. Let her talk her nonsense. What does it matter? I've got other things to think about than fruitless disputation with my one and only. She'll keep on yapping, she may in the coming months, years, become obsessive, send off for prospectuses from away-in-the-manager establishments, even visit one or two. But one day she'll come round to my way of thinking. I shall prevail. That's the way it is.

When I feel like it I'll tell Lily that I share her horror of the Comprehensive, that of course I've no intention of letting our babe trudge in his cousins' Adidas footsteps; of catching a school bus festooned with ads for Burger King, Toys R Us, Snickers; of drooping along corridors lined with signs for national brands and local companies, clutching books whose covers recommend Kellogg's Pop-Tarts and Sky TV personalities.

Lee showed us his homework recently: a classroom business course that teaches students the value of work by demonstrating how McDonald's restaurants are run.

Lily was aghast. 'This is unbelievable,' she said, but that was the least of it.

The children start their day not with a school assembly, and the religious indoctrination of our times, but go directly to their classrooms and watch a news programme, current events for teens, interspersed with commercials. Then they turn on their monitors, which greet them with the words, 'This computer was brought to you by Kentucky Fried Chicken. Have a nice day.'

'This is horrific,' Lily gasped.

'Darling,' I said, 'how many comprehensive schools do you imagine have a state-of-the-art computer for every single pupil? How could they afford it?'

As he saw the effect it had on this female member of his audience, Lee continued his account; he was enjoying himself.

'The Nike swoosh is painted on the roof,' he said. 'So that people in planes can see it. That paid for all our sports kits.'

Soda vending machines in the halls: that's how it began. Coca-Cola paid for a new gym, an electronic scoreboard on the basketball court. Exclusive vending rights. You can never stamp brand loyalty too young. With the next contract they offered more money to the school if it exceeded consumption of a given quota of Coke products in a year. Machines were installed along each corridor, on every landing. Pupils were allowed, encouraged, to drink Coke in the classroom: one Monday morning they found can holders attached to their desks.

'You don't have to ask Miss or Sir to be excused,' Lee said. 'They gave that up this term. You just leave.'

Lily was indignant. She tried to rouse the boys to action, to assert their right to freedom from such blatant propaganda.

Clint shrugged. 'It doesn't bother me,' he said. 'I had all that Coke shit, but hey, I prefer Pepsi.'

'Look,' I told Lily. 'Greg sent them there, as he vowed he would, but he saw what the facilities were like, so he joined the PTA; he was soon invited on to the School Board, and the next year he was elected Chair of the Governors.'

'Good for him,' she said.

'Yes, and he threw his energy into corporate sponsorship. He got his friend Terry Leckfield, you've met him, that bald guy, the new job of School Marketing Broker: on a percentage deal, no salary, no commitment from the school. And hey presto.'

'I don't like it,' she said.

'Neither do I,' I said. 'The first local partners bought advertising rights on the school railings, and public address announcements at football games. What their money paid for, at a time when other schools all over this country were losing playing fields left, right and centre, was a new soccer pitch with a stand and floodlights.'

She grimaced. 'I'm just not sure,' she said.

'Of course you're not,' I said. 'How could you be? But deals are made by people who don't dither. You know what?'

I stopped talking, so she shrugged irritably at me. 'Yes? What?'

'We were those first local corporate partners. *Spudnik* provided those facilities.'

She looked at me. Looked into me. She closed her eyes and looked away. 'You people,' she said.


The thing I have to remind myself about Lily is that she can argue remorselessly if she's in the mood, but as long as I concede particular, trivial, points, and not the whole argument, as long as I bide my time, in other words, and don't try to shout her down or turn my back or change the subject, I'll be surprised. What Lily wants is to express not a point of view, exactly, but her right to have a point of view. Usually this is enough to more or less satisfy her: once she's expressed sufficient opinion – often well-informed – Lily will quite suddenly say, 'OK! Have it your way! As long as you know what I think.'

I am the opposite. I've no need of discussion, in fact I'd

rather do without explaining myself. I'd rather be left to work out what to do, and do it.

I have never imagined that my wife fell head over heels in love with me. Did I say she did? Pure fantasy, if so. No, as I got to know her better, I became convinced that Lily loved someone else, has regarded someone else as her soulmate, someone she can't have for whatever reason. Which means for her that it's not possible to love anyone else equally. This is just a hunch, I don't even have a clear candidate for the position of lost love: it could be one of the lovers she's mentioned as we've shared our pasts, or it could be a secret or even an entirely unrequited affair.

I believe my wife has reconciled herself to this, to a life without extraordinary love. Maybe it's the memory of the person, of what they had or might have had, that sustains her; or maybe it's more a simple acceptance of life as it is, to be seen through and made the most of. She met me playing football, there was an agreeable tension between us. Conversation kicked and sparked. I had what looked to her like a reliable supply of money, we were each eager for children. In fact, I think we both surprised ourselves at the felicity of our meeting, the fit of our coming together – a warm handshake eliding into a deep kiss, a shag, an embracing hug – that amounted to something oddly solid, substantial.

The European Commission recently issued a directive allowing companies to apply for patents on human genes, microorganisms, and any plant or animal derived from a microbiological process.

'If these patent laws were available when chemists first identified the elements,' Lily told me, 'those chemists, or their patrons, could have patented them.'

'Surely not?'

'Everyone in the world would then have had to pay a royalty for the right to breathe in oxygen.'

I laughed. 'Sounds like someone wants to play God.'

Lily looked at me with what appeared to be real affection. 'Exactly,' she said.

'But what do you want?' I demanded. 'I mean, *you* people. What do you want?'

'Why can't we accept ourselves as we are?'

'What are we?' I asked her back.

Lily smiled at me. 'Beautiful, flawed beings,' she said.

'Yes,' I said. 'That's right.'

'We're not perfectible.'

'Of course we are,' I said. 'Eternally so.'

I'm nuts about my wife. Did I mention that, already? Call me uxorious, I just happen to think she's gorgeous, and I'm not alone. The only one who thinks she isn't is herself. She believes she has lopsided breasts. She stands in front of the mirror and says towards me, 'Look. You see?'

'You have lopsided *eyes*, darling,' I tell her. Am I going to lie? She thinks she's put on weight, too, and she has: she used to be scrawny. I get older, the more I like something to get hold of. The more woman I like. The more flesh.

There's been a bone of contention between Lily and me recently: over the baby. She wants Jacob in bed with us at night. I don't disagree – it's a great idea! I know some men feel the child as a literal wedge between them and their spouses but really, such jealousy is incredibly immature, isn't it? Me, I find the presence of this fat little human being, with his warm skin, not to mention my wife's spreading figure, has brought an amplitude of sensuality. An increased eroticisation of the marital bed, somehow. Let's be honest, can any woman suck one's finger like a baby? No wonder some women come when they breastfeed. Feeling his limbs connecting ours, watching his extraordinary suck on my wife's nipple, my carnal desire for her intensifies.

At the same time, it's true, a baby is a cute contraceptive. But why get upset about it? It doesn't take a man a minute to relieve his libido.

No, the point at issue is not us, it's him: John Junior doesn't seem to me to sleep as well beside his mother as away from her. If I take him to a spare room and only bring him back to Lily for feeding (yes, me with a draining day ahead, do I need this, people ask, such disruption? Surely we could afford a wise gnarled nanny; a nubile au pair; a housekeeper from a poverty-stricken country, ugly and devoted? Those shadow occupants of wealthy homes? I'm sure we could) then John Junior will sleep still and silent for three hours between feeds – as does Lily.

When he spends the whole night beside his mother, however, John J. snuffles and snorts in his sleep, half-wakes and, smelling her milky breasts there, demands feeding. She is woken, and feeds him. I tell her he's sluicing fresh milk down his gullet to only half-digested milk in his stomach. She does agree that he only sucks plentifully after three hours' sleep or more.

Most of Lily's friends leave their babies to cry in their own room at night until they realise there's no point in crying and lie down again. Sleep training. Obtain decent nights for themselves so they can get back to work or, as my wife puts it, get back to paying their mortgage. She knows how unlucky they are, how lucky she is; which she resents, of course, but that's another matter. She doesn't need or want to get back to work.

Sleep training, then, is the prevailing orthodoxy, and Lily fights it. She says our son wants to be close to us, that separation is cruel: it answers the parents' needs, not the baby's.

'We've spent a million years sleeping together,' she claims. 'We must be mad to have stopped.'

She quotes anthropological examples at me. Dwindling tribes whose parents hoick their kids on hip, in sling, all day long, and bundle up *en famille* at night. The examples are almost archaeological, the reason for which Lily unwittingly alludes to even as she cites them. 'Indulgent parents,' she says, 'babies who are listened to. They make gentle societies.'

'I believe it,' I say, omitting to point out that her gentle, isolated tribes are forever disappearing. The empires of our age are harsh towards their children. Look around. We're aggressive, and successful. I say nothing. I don't want John J. to grow up a lout; let our sons and daughters share our beds, I tell Lily.

John Junior loves to kick: in the bath, or lying on his back with his naked legs in the air. And his hands, the way he moves his fingers in the air sometimes, he makes me think of a pianist flexing his fingers. About to play.

A letter arrived amongst the post I took up on Lily's breakfast tray the other Saturday morning, addressed not to her or to me but to our son. It was a copy of one he gets sent regularly to remind his guardians – us – that he's overdue his immunisation. Less than five months old and he should have had a skinful of jabs by now: three single-dose injections for Hib and three triple doses for diphtheria, whooping cough and tetanus. Pincushions, his dimply upper arms and fleshy outer thighs! Not to mention three doses of polio vaccine administered by mouth, revolting drops on his tongue.

My wife is adamant in her refusal of all persuasion from the medical establishment – including, she claims, her GP threatening to strike us as a family off her register.

'She practically accused me of child abuse,' Lily said. 'But the fact is she's paid a bonus when she reaches a target of babies immunised in her practice.'

'That's serious pressure,' I said.

'She's afraid I'd influence other parents, too.'

'A virus of resistance.'

'Look,' Lily told me. 'While I'm breastfeeding him, he has my maternal immunity. To measles, mumps and rubella at least. And chicken pox. It's *because* I got those childhood ailments that I can protect our son from them.'

'Honey,' I said, 'diseases that once crippled and killed countless children have been eradicated in this country.'

'Yes, through clean drinking water. Proper drains. Decent diet. You told me yourself how potato consumption abolished scurvy.'

'Come on. Partly through a comprehensive childhood immunisation programme.'

Lily nodded ironically. 'Sure. Last time there was a campaign to immunise all children up to the age of sixteen with the measles and rubella vaccine – all kids, mind, even those who'd already *had* their supposedly full series of jabs – to prevent a forthcoming epidemic.'

'Yes? What about it?'

'Eight million doses were administered.'

'That's a lot of children. It sounds like a comprehensive amount to me.'

'Supplied by a single drug company. It turned out the entire batch just happened to be approaching its sell-by date. It *had* to be used, or thrown away.'

My wife munched her toast, sipped her tea, between sentences. Our son was at her breast the whole time. She's amazing. I sighed. 'Where on earth do you get your facts from, darling? Don't tell me. That homeopath friend of yours? Or what's her name – the astrologer?' About large corporations, pharmaceutical ones in particular, Lily is valiantly cynical. Oh yes, of rational, provable science she's relentlessly sceptical. Only the flakey stuff does she take at face value.

'We all got measles when we were kids, John. Didn't we? Chicken pox. Don't you remember? One of the problems with this whole thing is these vaccines wear off – and people are then contracting what would have been mild childhood diseases as teenagers, or adults. When they're not mild at all.'

'It's a complicated subject,' I kind of allowed. 'You know what we need, don't you?'

'What?'

'It's clear. *Safe* vaccines.'

Lily frowned. 'I suppose.'

Yes. That's right. Safe vaccines. We're going to supply them. We're going to make real money. We are. Simon and I have planned the future. At the moment you take your child to the clinic for a vaccine for measles, mumps, rubella, the nice cruel nurse administers a jab in your little one's thigh, making him or her cry, leaving a lump under the skin. The defilement. No longer. Have a spoonful of mashed potato. Here, child, eat a chip. I see government contracts. Honours. Money.

What do you know, I may even get around to doing some of the renovation that crumbling millstone of a house of ours desperately needs.

While day slowly dawns outside I can be found lying in the spare bed beside John Junior with a mug of coffee. Smooth Colombian. I need it, I'm yawning, when John J.'s had a bad night. And you don't know what a bad night is until you've had a baby. It's one of the banal revelations awaiting. There are others. To be honest, I wouldn't mind apologising to those acquaintances over the years who'd say of their crying infants, 'I wonder if she wants a feed now?' or 'Does he want to have a walk in the sling?'

I'd think, How can you not know, you idiot, isn't it straightforward enough for you? How much more simple could it be than this tiny blob of primal needs? He/she/it needs to eat and excrete and sleep and, yes, to be caressed and held and entertained. I mean, if the babe's unhappy you have a limited number of choices. Choose!

Or the odd occasions I've waited to go for a walk with someone with a toddler, I've stood outside fuming to myself, For Christ's sake, we said we'd leave at ten, it's half past already, what are you people doing in there? Get the kid, put it in the buggy, let's go!

Now I know better and I'd like to say sorry, I really would. I want to pop back in time and find those people in their hallways, wrestling with nappies and clothes and recalcitrant limbs, and hats and strollers and aching shoulders, and say, 'Hey, I know that was me standing outside cursing, me the single man, the callow bachelor, in case you picked up the vibe, but *the real me* is here now to apologise for him, he knows nothing.'

Or the years Greg came in to work hollow-eyed, unable to converse the way we had before his kids came: disembodied and distracted. Now I know. That nights can be eternal, hours become epochs, ages of sleeplessness. In the night, however torrid it is, you know you'll have to drag yourself sluggish through the next day. This thought is with you, and with hundreds, thousands of fellow parents all over the country walking around their living rooms in an endless soothing circuit, or bumping the baby up and down stairs, or administering fingers dipped in fennel, or pushing their pram along the streets, or driving around the block, or standing helpless above the cots of their colicky, gripe-stricken, squalling beloveds.

Short-tempered men are forced to dig into their unknown

selves, to mine hidden reserves of patience deep in their characters. Selfish women who thought all sacrifice was a sign of weakness find themselves called upon to give, and are surprised by a thin sediment of joy lurking at the bottom of exhaustion. How many fail, and cast their children loose and unprotected into the storms of the life ahead, but not all, no. In the dead of night, invisible in dim bedrooms, unnoticed by history, such heroism, such sacrifice, is being offered. And what do you know? It's my turn now!

But how long a night lasts with a baby. The blanket of night becomes subdivided – the hours separate from one another – into chunks of specific activity: John J. sleeps a couple of hours, then wakes, and feeds for forty-five minutes. Sits up wide-eyed and playful for one hour, becomes tired, dopey but fractious as he creeps slowly back to the edge of sleep over the course of half an hour until he drops off in my arms, on Lily's shoulder, one or other of our fingers in his mouth. He then dreams peacefully for an hour before beginning to fret in his sleep, and this is the worst time, the worst of the mini-epochs of the night: when John Junior grunts and groans, brings his knees up to his chest, snuffles and grumbles, shakes his little head, brings clenched fists up to his face. It's impossible to sleep beside him. We lift him up, put him on our chests, move him on to his side, his back, his front. Nothing really helps much, except the welcome splurt and rumble in his nappy. Until finally he wakes, and so begins the next cycle.

Whereas once anything less than seven hours' uninterrupted unconsciousness left one unnourished and grouchy, now the night breaks up and sleep comes in rich nuggets, each one filled with the nutrients of oblivion. Woken by the baby's wail you check the figures on the luminous alarm clock and say to your wife, who has herself been woken moments earlier by her tumid breasts, 'Two thirty. That's over three hours.' And you can feel the bounty of all those two hundred minutes of deep sleep in your loosened head, swollen limbs, rested cells.

Shopping for the baby before it was born drove Lily crazy. Don't get me wrong, she wanted everything for him, but the sheer quantity of choice oppressed her. Slings and Wilkinets and backpacks. Prams and pushchairs, strollers and joggers and buggies. Carrycots and car seats. It was less the difficulty of choosing that irritated her, more, simply, the wasteful existence of so wide a variety of objects.

But I mustn't draw a picture of my pregnant wife as an angry harridan. Last autumn was warm, at night we lay glued together. When it cooled down we canoodled like teenagers. And I made Lily laugh like never before, I can't describe how, from silly slapstick with my lanky body. Pregnancy made her susceptible to humour, and she farted with laughter. She enjoyed what her body was doing.

I remember, though, one evening a little over a year ago we were arguing about the same kind of thing as the baby-stuff choice. This would be about the time our son was made. Maybe the very moment. Lily was banging on about the iniquities of free trade again.

'Listen,' I said. 'Globalisation is what makes all this possible.'

'All what possible?' she demanded.

*Our lives*, I could have said, but I needed to convince her with specifics. 'All this,' I said, pincering the hem of my jacket between thumb and forefinger. I was clutching at straws. I wrestled myself free of the jacket. It was a gamble, I knew that. 'Look,' I said, triumphantly relieved. '*Made in Italy.*'

'Yes?' she said. 'And what does that prove? Precisely?'

She was right. It was a partial victory, no victory at all.

A glance made me realise I stood a better chance with her: she was wearing her usual mix of clothes, bought from a combination of ethnic shops and sports outfitters. Floppy cottons and wools in bright colours, and tight manmade monochromes.

'One sample proves nothing,' I said, advancing towards her. 'For a study of this nature, we need at least ten separate items of data.'

Before she knew what was going on I'd lifted her arms up straight above her head – where, taken by surprise, they unnaturally remained, holding up an invisible ceiling – and I grabbed the bottom of the green and orange sweater she had on. I shimmied it up her torso. I think if I'd been able to accomplish the theft in one clean sweep she'd have let me, but her next layer down was a fleecy thing upon which the sweater got fraught. I'd only managed to pull the bottom of it up over her face when her muffled voice exclaimed, 'Hey! What are you up to?' As she dropped her arms. 'What do you think you're doing?'

My wife complains that I have tunnel vision, and it's true: once I start something, I'm constitutionally incapable of giving up on it, of allowing it to remain unfinished. I kept pulling the jumper up Lily's chest and arms, tugging it over her squirming protestations. As I pulled she, fortunately, backed away from me, which only played into my hands: the orange and green pullover sprang free towards me.

My wife staggered a step or two as she regained her balance. 'Did you just do what I think you did?' she gasped.

I ignored her, knowing I had to forestall either the presumption of my assault, or my victory in the ensuing tug-of-war, becoming an issue: I went straight for the label.

'Look!' I said.

Still recovering, Lily was unsure yet whether to respond to my general behaviour or this specific command.

'See!' I said, thrusting the label towards her.

'*Made in Guatemala*,' she read aloud. 'So?'

'You wouldn't be able to wear a sweater like this if it wasn't for globalisation.'

She looked at me with the contempt I deserved. 'Wake up, man,' she said and, taking the sweater from me, looked into each of its sleeves, and then inside its hem. 'Well, it doesn't say so here but it said on the tag, they're made by a women's co-operative.'

We stared at each other for a moment. 'I'll have to take your word for it,' I acceded, but even as I did so I was neatly unpicking my tie and sliding it loose from around my neck. As I peered at the label, she leaned in and did so too.

'See?' she exclaimed in triumph. '*Made in England*.'

'Precisely! Exported all over the world,' I countered. 'Anyway, the point is, and this is the point: what's it made of?'

'*Pure silk*,' she read.

'And where does the silk come from?' I asked.

She didn't know the answer, but I guess she did know it wasn't going to help her. Instead she began furiously to unbutton my shirt. 'Right. OK,' she said. 'My turn.' Standing square in front of me she fiddled the buttons out from their eyeholes as if my shirt were on fire and, as the front flapped loose, she reached up and grabbed both ends of the collar and yanked the shirt down my bare back. The sleeves ruffled down my arms, only to bunch at the wrists.

Thwarted by cufflinks, my wife cursed – 'Shit!' – but she instantly spotted an opening: she reached both her arms behind me and scrunched the body of my shirt into as tight a wad as she could and said, 'You're stuck.' A childish smile invaded her face. 'You're stuck and I'm right,' Lily breathed at me.

What an elegant example of intuitive logic. It's true,

I *was* stuck, my arms were pinned to my sides. I happened to have been trapped by my own cufflinks and my wife took this as proof that my intellectual position was flawed.

In reaching around behind me, Lily had pressed her body against me. I could feel with my penis, through the thin and skintight layers of clothing between us, the shape of her pubic mound.

'You haven't even checked the label,' I said.

She let go of one hand and waltzed around behind me, regathering the shirt when she got there. Having missed a momentary opportunity of escape I now tried, too late, to move my hands, but – other than inwards, as if to applaud my captor – it was surprisingly impossible. Not without an authentic violent tussle, anyway.

'Guess,' she said.

'Thailand,' I tried.

'Wrong. *One hundred per cent cotton*,' she intoned.

'What, is that a clue?'

'No. Not really. I already guessed, by the way.'

'What do you mean you guessed?'

'You've got one more go.'

'Malaysia,' I said.

'No.' She let go of the shirt and I felt her fingers grip my left cuff and slide it out over my wrist, then do the same to the right. 'I guessed India,' she said, as I turned around, and she handed the shirt to me.

I looked at the label. It said, *Made in India*. Her eyes were still shiny with that childish glee, convinced she'd turned the tables on me.

'Well, if that's the way you're going to play this,' I said, and I reached forward and took the catch of the zip of her charcoal fleece vest. Gripping the hem of the vest with my left hand, I smartly unzipped her.

'I'm armless underneath,' she said.

'I don't think so,' I smiled, and slid the vest off her acquiescent body. 'It says it's a Flyer. *Made in USA.*'

'But by *Patagonia*,' she said.

'Exactly,' I said. 'I remember their website. You showed me.' Lily has a car sticker, bought from one of those Outdoor Clothes and Accessories outlets she likes, that proclaims:

### Screw the Net. Surf the Backcountry.

But she orders most of such clothes from internet shops.

'Right,' she said. 'They're a company started and run by people who live the outdoor life.' She squatted down and untied my shoelaces.

'When they're not living the executive life,' I said, stepping out of my hand-stitched shoes.

'That has nothing, zero, zilch to do with globalisation,' she said. 'These shoes were *Made in Portugal*, by the by. Plus, anyway, *Patagonia*'s cotton is one hundred per cent organic.'

'You left the info-label attached,' I said. 'Listen to this: *A lightweight technical pullover that provides exceptional warmth with minimal bulk and weight. Ideal for a great variety of activities, from providing core insulation on technical outdoor adventures to keeping warm at the beach when the sun goes down. Slim fit through the hips minimizes conflict with harnesses and hipbelts. Anatomically engineered for women.*'

Some job: anatomical engineer for women's second skins. Call me a pervert if you will, but am I the only person this kind of thing turns on? Lily, meanwhile, was unrolling my socks.

'*As with all of our products,*' I continued, '*our fleece garments are engineered with the same ideology* – ideology! who said it was dead? – *the same ideology of minimum weight and bulk with maximum performance. We have*

130

*utilized some of the most innovative fabrics in the world to ensure incredible freedom of movement for high mobility and activity. And a close comfortable fit that maximizes warmth to weight ratios.'*

As Lily stood up I lowered myself to one knee, grasping the top of her thermal leggings on the way down: as she rose, I peeled them down her legs.

'They donate a percentage of their profits to environmental groups,' she said.

'They can afford it,' I said. 'Their profits are vast. They're a corporation. They're worth millions. And why not? There's nothing wrong with that.'

My wife, leaning forward, put her hands on my shoulders for balance. I pulled the leggings off her lifting feet. They had the feel of an underground nocturnal animal; I brought them to my face and breathed in her heat and her aroma.

'Dakini,' I said. '*Made in USA* as well. *Holders of the Crazy Wisdom*, it says. Buddhist tights, no less.'

She grasped my neck just below my ears and ushered me up. As I rose I took her pink sleeveless T-shirt with me: this time she leaned forward to hurry its removal, and stayed there to unclip my belt and unzip my flies. The trousers crumpled to the floor. I stepped out of them as I grabbed her hair, and squeezed handfuls of it. She'd yanked my briefs down and took my throbbing cock in her mouth. I could have come quicker than either of us wanted.

'No,' I said, pulling her off me. I leaned over her back and undid her bra, holding the undone catch in place till I'd encouraged her upright again before letting the bra go, so that I could watch the spilling release of her gorgeous breasts. I put a hand on the back of her head and pulled us together and kissed her while with the other hand I eased down her knickers by clumsy degrees. We lowered ourselves to the floor then, where I abandoned her mouth and rotated my way around to her quim. It was waiting for me. She returned to my cock.

That's how it was for us. That's the kind of thing we did. I don't suppose we shall again. But who knows? Who knows?

# Dry Rot

Externally, skin wrinkled; concentric
rings around infected area and white,
pink or blue-green pustules present.
Internally, cavities often with fluffy mycelium.
Boundary between healthy and
diseased areas indistinct.

# MONDAY 12.45 P.M.

I DRIVE around, around the ring road, at fifty-five. I feel as if I'm tethered to the centre of town by a long rope, like a horse. Every car should be broken in this way.

The more I consider the matter, the less I think there should be any fuss at all. Two aboriginal villagers who were possibly ill already, their deaths unrelated to the peripheral role they played in the AlphaGen trial. I really do think Simon is overreacting. I'll calm him down, and I'll calm Greg down too when I tell him. And I will tell him.

Here comes the turn-off for . . . Grove Wildlife Park. Stoke Abbey. Brown signs, the heritage colour. They're everywhere now. Brown signs used to be allowed only for country houses and zoos and whatnot that attracted a minimum of visitors, say twenty thousand a year. Until a bright spark in the Treasury realised, hey, that doesn't make any money. So now they're simply sold. If a person wants a brown heritage sign they just buy it.

Look, here comes another one: for a pub. The White Hart at Newbridge. They do good food there. I feel a bit peckish. Almost lunchtime, what time is it?

I know about the brown signs because Greg said a couple of years ago, when we were trying to sort out a cash-flow problem, 'Why don't we open up the site here to visitors? Charge entrance?'

'You what?' I said.

'Offer them cream teas, ice creams, a guided tour.'

'A tour of what?'

'The potatoes' journey. In on the lorries, off on the loaders. Sorters and packers, right through the warehouse. The graders.'

I shook my head sadly at my brother.

'They'd love it,' Greg said, even while shrugging the idea loose from his shoulders and letting it go as he walked out of my office. Idiotic. Although actually I think he was on to something. Men love to watch other men working, don't they? Roadworkers, window cleaners, builders: look around and you invariably find other chaps idly studying them.

Greg said to me, when I first mentioned AlphaGen's business to him, 'What are you telling me all this about bananas for?'

'Bananas,' I said, 'illustrate the process of bio-pharming. We deal in potatoes, but we need to think of them as a particular technology. Different markets require appropriate technologies.'

The principle remains the same. Food that provides nutrition and medicine in the same mouthful. Bananas are a common food staple in most of those countries whose children are dying needlessly. They don't need to be refrigerated. They're customarily eaten raw. A field is cheaper than a chemical manufacturing plant. There is no need for sterile equipment nor trained medical personnel.

Greg was squeezing his mobile as if urging it to interrupt us. 'And consider this,' I told him. 'By engineering a few pigmentation genes, the medicinal bananas could have their peel splashed a different colour from normal ones. The blue bananas are good for you.'

Greg emitted a dismissive burp of laughter. 'No shit.'
'Pink potatoes will make you well.'

Before bearing a child, ought we to ask ourselves whether
we should be adding another mouth to the population of
this world? I was in town a couple of weeks ago. I saw
the beggars. Asylum seekers. Drug addicts. Should we be
inflicting this world upon a new being?

But I don't have to justify myself to Greg or anyone else.
That's the beauty of the times we live in.

Lily's pregnancy was what they call an easy one. A
minimum of morning sickness, no apparent complications.
We were well monitored. She had ultra-sound scans. At
seventeen weeks her midwife reckoned she was too big.
'Either we're a month out with our calculations,' she
told Lily, 'or there are twins gathering there.' Twins!
We thought, My God, it's cloned itself! Over the week
between this assessment and the resultant scan I took to
the idea. I'd like us to have a couple of children, and what
could be better than both at once?

Lily lay down, I sat beside her, the radiographer slapped
on some cool gunk and moved her scanning device over
my wife's gelid tummy. We watched a churning, mercu-
rial flux on the black and white monitor. It looked like
ancient footage, from some nineteenth-century archive. A
primitive, spooky attempt at photographic representation.
Opaque prenatal images.

'There's the head,' the technician said. 'There's a
foot.'

All I could see was a bubbly, blobby cauldron. Maybe in
fact it was quite clear, and I was like one of those natives
given a photograph who turns it round and upside down.
I just couldn't see the new.

'But how many are there?' my wife asked.

'How many? Just the one,' the technician said. 'Look, there's its arm.'

*What happened to the other one?* I wanted to ask. *What have you done with our twin?* I almost demanded in sudden disappointment. Then I saw the baby's back: the interlocking vertebrae in its curved bent spine, emerging through the murk; bones brand new, and prehistoric.

Lily dragged me along to antenatal classes, although she'd already read the books: she knew everything the midwife and health visitor told us. The most useful thing they could have got us to do would have been to tie one hand behind our backs and try making a cup of tea. Because with a baby in the other hand that's what you'll soon be doing. One-handed games would be a good ice-breaker, actually, in a circle of belly-protruding, queenly women – beside each, in comparison, a weedy-looking man-drone. All our lives about to be turned inside out. Anxious, smug, serious women. It was comic.

Lily planned a home birth, to which her gynaecologist shrugged in a Mediterranean way and said, 'No problem.' We prepared the house as if for a party, music all set up – belly dance tapes to help with contractions, Bach and Enya in between. Fairy lights and incense. Bowls and towels and whatnot. We almost hired a birthing pool, some friends of hers had used one. The bloke shed his clothes and jumped in too. Lily's a dolphin in water, and perhaps for that reason she didn't like the idea of being trapped in a pool of it for hours.

The baby was due on the 3rd of December, but the first one's generally late, and ours duly was. The following Friday Lily had an appointment with the midwife, and while she was in the surgery she had a show, as it's called: a discharge of blood as the mucus plug that keeps the amniotic sac protected, at the neck of the cervix, comes loose; the first sign of the onset of childbirth. Propitious timing, we thought. Lily came home excited, and sure enough, around midnight her contractions started.

We called the midwives in the morning and the senior one came at 9 a.m. She's been practising in and around town for forty years; she's delivered the babies of people we know, not to mention the people themselves. She gave Lily an internal examination and pronounced that there was no dilation of the cervix yet. It needs to dilate ten centimetres before a woman's ready to give birth. Lily's contractions continued. The midwife came back at 1 p.m., performed another vaginal examination, and said the cervix was still barely open.

The rest of Saturday afternoon, into the evening, and all through the night Lily had regular, painful contractions.

'They're not right,' she told me. 'I knew they were going to be painful, but this is the wrong pain.'

'How can you be sure?' I asked her.

'Look,' she said, holding her fingers against the front of her lower abdomen. We consulted diagrams. 'It's pushing out against my synthesis pubis. It should be pushing down against the cervix.' She grimaced as another contraction came. 'It's not right.' She closed her eyes, she looked tired.

'I'll phone,' I said.

At 3 a.m. an on-call midwife came. She gave Lily another internal. 'It's barely one finger dilated,' she said. 'If that. Why don't you take a couple of paracetamol, get your husband here to make you a hot-water bottle, and try and get some sleep.'

It was good advice, and we took it, and Lily slept a few hours. She woke, but carried on dozing on and off through Sunday morning, until the contractions started again around noon, immediately painful, stabbing her, in the same way as they had before.

She spoke on the phone to someone, I don't remember whether it was a doctor or a midwife, and they said to relax as much as possible and just stay with it. We had the feeling we were going round in circles. Sunday evening wasn't too bad, and Lily got some rest, but then from midnight on she was in a lot of pain, with the same short, sharp contractions.

Lily sent me to the spare room to get some sleep. 'You won't help me if you're exhausted,' she said.

Around the middle of Monday the contractions became longer and more regular than they had been. Another midwife, an Irishwoman, came at 3 p.m. She gave my wife an internal examination and said the cervix had thinned, it had just started to dilate.

'This has been going on since Friday night, for Christ's sake,' I said.

'It's not the right pain,' Lily insisted. But I could see that the midwife didn't heed what she was saying, because she was in such control. 'It's really painful,' my wife said, but she wasn't weeping and wailing so the midwives just thought, *This woman, she doesn't know what pain is – but she will soon enough, God help her*.

The Irish midwife advised Lily to rest, to lie on her left side, which meant the baby's back would be facing downwards, and gravity might encourage his head away from where it seemed to be hurting her. I took the midwife aside as she left. 'Tell me,' I whispered through gritted teeth, 'what the hell is going on?'

'It's fine,' she said. 'Everything is fine. You relax as well yourself.'

Lily lay on her side but the searing pain continued striking her. At 1 a.m. we called the hospital and yet another midwife turned up. Her vaginal examination revealed dilation of barely three centimetres. She stayed with us, calm as all the others. At two-thirty all of a sudden my wife's waters broke. There was a smell like the smell of a broken egg. Over the following three and a half hours Lily had intermittently strong and weak contractions. Still that pain.

'We'll do another examination at six,' Vicky promised. Our anticipation prickled: when the time came all three of us were eager. Vicky felt around. You could see her trying to stop herself frowning. 'I'm afraid there's no further dilation.'

We were getting desperate by now. Lily started trembling. She tried walking up and down the stairs to jog the baby loose, with little effect on anything except to tire her further, so she took a couple of paracetamol and we both went to bed, while downstairs Vicky swapped shifts with the next midwife and explained my wife's situation. But Lily couldn't sleep. She was still suffering stabbing pain with every useless contraction, and I could feel her shaking beside me. 'I can't stop,' she said. 'I have to stop trembling. Run me a hot bath.'

I did as she asked. 'It's no good, John,' she stuttered. 'We have to go to hospital. Let me have the bath, help me stop shaking, and then we'll sort this out.'

The hot bath helped. I got tea and biscuits on a tray and Lily came downstairs, and we sat with Jenny the new midwife.

'I realise it's not happening,' my wife said. She was still so calm, though she'd hardly slept now for eighty hours, except for sporadic dozes, and suffered a great deal of pain. I was as proud of her as I was worried.

'No, it's not,' Jenny agreed.

'I wanted a home birth, but that's OK,' my wife said. 'Let's go to the hospital.'

'Yes, I agree,' Jenny said. 'Let's go now.'

Jenny drove up to the hospital, we followed. At eleven, Tuesday morning, Jenny booked us into a delivery suite. An anaesthetist, in a light blue uniform that exactly matched his deep sea eyes, came and put a drip in the back of my wife's left hand, ready for oxytocin, which induces contractions, and also for a rehydrating fluid called Hartmann's solution. Then he inserted a neat epidural into her lower back.

By twelve-thirty Lily announced that the epidural was working, which meant she was no longer troubled by the peculiar agony of her contractions. At last. A breakthrough. Jenny told us to try and sleep. I closed my eyes in the plastic armchair and sank straight into bottomless dreams. My insane wife didn't sleep at all.

At two, Jenny added the oxytocin drip, and the afternoon slipped and bobbed along, with Jenny adjusting the oxytocin intake to optimise contractions: those hours have disappeared into a black hole of time. At six, Jenny gave Lily a vaginal examination and announced that there was full dilation. To say I was relieved would be something of an understatement.

'We'll start delivery in one hour,' Jenny said.

We were relaxed and confident. I felt so sorry for Lily. She'd planned a birth in which she would be in control, walking around the house, swaying her hips to music she liked. Here she was virtually strapped down, with an epidural stuck into her spine, an oxytocin drip feeding into her hand, and monitors attached to her belly that measured muscular movement i.e. the contractions of her uterus, and showed them on a screen. While a further device measured the baby's heartbeat, indicated on a second screen.

'Don't worry,' she said. 'I feel stronger, free of that pain. I feel I'll be able to do whatever I need to.'

We watched the build-up of contractions on the monitor and at seven Lily started pushing with them, expecting like the midwife a quick third stage, and the imminent emergence of our child. Every five minutes or so we'd see the line on the screen start jumping and I'd say to my wife, 'Now!' and she pushed the way she'd been preparing for, exerting all her might.

Nothing happened. Time went by. At eight o'clock Vicky, the midwife from the night before, came on shift and joined us. Jenny could have left but she said no, she'd stay with us. On her own time. Vicky was good, she encouraged Lily to go for it, and my wife was pushing brilliantly, three times with every contraction. Jenny and now Vicky felt around inside her; they could feel the baby's head, they couldn't work out why it wasn't coming around the pubic bone and out. I looked too. I could see the top of the baby's head, and I could see that Lily's pushing, despite what must have been her exhaustion, was exerting tremendous force. But the baby just wouldn't, couldn't, emerge.

At eight forty-five Jenny said, very calmly, 'I think I'll just go and have a chat with a doctor.'

I realised Jenny had been keeping an eye on the screen that monitored the baby's heartbeat, watching out for signs of foetal distress. I didn't have any idea that it was also being watched by doctors on a matching screen in a central office in the middle of the delivery suites. Jenny came back with a male doctor. I think he was Dutch. He examined my wife, and, also very calmly, suggested he use a ventouse, a vacuum extractor, to help the baby out.

Lily agreed, and then, all of a sudden, everything changed: our quiet room was invaded by doctors in masks, nurses pushing trolleys, orderlies carrying equipment. Leads, wires, everywhere. Someone stepped forward and removed the end of the bed and stirrups were clicked into place, and my wife's feet strapped into them. We'd been plunged into the centre of a medical emergency.

A semi-circle of medics grouped themselves around the end of my wife's bed. Two doctors. A paediatrician with a trolley bearing an infra-red lamp over a tiny cot. An anaesthetist. A nurse. One of our midwives.

I stood on one side of the bed by my wife's left shoulder, Jenny by her right.

The Dutch doctor injected an anaesthetic into my wife's perineum, and he emptied her bladder with a catheter tube. An assistant then started up the vacuum of the ventouse machine, and the doctor attached the end, which looked like a sink plunger, to the baby's visible head.

Encouraged by all, my wife pushed in time to the monitors' urgings. She gave it her all, and so did the Dutch doctor, pulling for all his worth on the ventouse. The baby's head began to emerge. The doctor grunted, Lily groaned. Like ringside fans, the rest of us cheered them on. Suddenly the suction on the baby's head snapped loose, the doctor staggered backwards across the room and the baby disappeared back inside where it'd clearly decided it was going to stay.

The doctor picked himself up. Everyone regrouped. The vacuum machine was started up again, the doc attached his toilet plunger, we all watched the screen, the lines started jumping.

'Now!' we cried. 'Push!' and my obedient, plucky wife pushed, and the doctor pulled. The baby's head came out, there it was, crowning, no doubt about it . . . Another inch! Come on! . . . When – plop! – again the ventouse came off, the doctor threw himself backwards, the baby retreated.

How long can this malarkey continue? I wondered. They're going to have to cut her open. Maybe the kid's weirdly malformed and there's an aberrational part of its unfortunate body hooked up in there. They warned us that was possible. What's it going through, anyway? When the hell are they going to decide to perform a Caesarian?

They started the palaver again though, went through it all, the same cries of encouragement, the same pushing and pulling. This time, the suction held, but even so the Dutch doctor didn't seem able to pull the child out, when suddenly my wife made a great grunting roar and pushed her baby's head clear out, and then the rest of its body slithered free. *Spontaneous vaginal delivery*, as the notes would confirm. The doctor made to pass him to the paediatrician, but Jenny assessed that he was OK and like a rugby player she intercepted, grabbed the baby and put him straight on to Lily's tummy.

Lily was done in. She was dazed. The medics administered syntometrine and pulled the placenta out, and they gave her a few stitches. I sat with her and hugged her and the baby, who was all dopey. His head smelled like honey and piss. John Junior had joined us.

'I DON'T know,' I told the doctor, 'I always seem to have a sore throat nowadays.'

'You think it's something in the air?'

'Me? I have no idea. Yes, maybe. What, do you think there is?'

'I don't know either. People say so, but I'm not qualified to comment. Your son, is he beginning to speak?'

'My son?' I laughed. 'No, of course not. Well, he's making noises, yes. Burbles. Squeaks. But not words. Perhaps one could say he's finding his voice.'

'And you're losing yours.'

'What? You think?' I shook my head. 'No.'

'Tell me more,' the doctor said. 'Tell me about the constipation.'

'Yes.' I shifted uneasily in my seat. 'Yes. Sometimes I do get the urge to defecate, well, I have that lovely ache in the arse, I don't know where it is exactly, you tell me, Doctor, and I make my way to the toilet. Only for the promised relief to, I don't know, retreat. No, to evaporate. Yes, for the putative stool to reveal itself as so much hot air. As wind, the sound of its expulsion amplified by the toilet bowl, which with its water is apparently a perfectly constructed acoustic instrument: a sardonic echo chamber. Mocking me.'

The doctor frowned. 'Do you think you're being a little, shall we say, melodramatic?'

'There's another thing.'

'Yes?'

'God. Yes. I'm embarrassed. Sometimes when I have had a shit it seems I can't clean myself. However much I wipe. I miss something. Roll off more pieces of tissue paper. Spinning the toilet-roll holder like a mouse in a cage. You know the places in the world where they don't use paper? They use water. They think what we do is unclean. They're right. I use more paper, enough to clog the U-bend. But a second flush and away it goes. All that soggy wadded mess of tissue, hurtling along the enduring drains.'

The doctor sat there, placid, impassive as ever.

I shook my head. 'Crazy,' I said. 'I remind myself of my mother. For fuck's sake.'

Y OU KNOW, everything is speeding up. Yes, except for my digestion, which is slowing down. Very funny. The last time I was in Berlin I had this taxi driver. He drove with one hand glued to the gearstick, the other alternately wrenching the steering wheel and fist-shaking at other cars. He was the most aggressive driver I've ever been driven by, and anyone who's been a passenger in my brother's Jaguar would appreciate what a tribute that is. This German punched the steering wheel, cursed, gave the finger to lorries and motorbikers.

At pedestrians he yelled (I translate), 'Get off za fucking pavement you shithound!' as he mounted the kerb in order to gain a few seconds. This lunatic tail-gated the car in front of him, jumped traffic lights, cut across lanes, beeping and snarling all the while. And I, sat in the back, was an irrelevant, if enthralled, witness. His passengers were less people than batons he picked up in a never-ending relay; an endless race through the traffic, a race he never wins for he is thwarted at every turn by incompetent fools.

A couple of weeks after John J. was born everyone came over to our place. We thought we'd do without a christening. We don't want godparents. Poor Lily. No immediate family of her own left, mobbed by the Sharpe menagerie.

'What you want mate's a Compaq iPAQ pocket PC,' Greg was informing Bill.

'I don't need games, mind.'

'Who does?'

'One or two, maybe.'

Lily and I sat on the sofa with John J. on our laps and let my family pay homage. 'He's beautiful, John,' said Melody. 'I'm so pleased.'

'It's Lily we should thank,' said Greg. 'If you'd left it much later, mind, love, he'd be supporting you all on his pension.'

'I'll support us if needs be, thanks, Greg,' Lily told him.

'I think it's very nineteenth century, John,' said Bill. Whatever the hell that meant.

Melody had brought cakes and persuaded Lily to stay put and let her fetch tea and squash from the kitchen, assisted by her children, who when she asked them to help rose as one with robotic good grace.

Since her fall before Christmas, Mum zimmer frames around her bungalow, but she's got a wheelchair for special occasions. She can operate it herself with a joystick but being pushed makes her feel more important. Lee was lumbered with the job.

'Watch my ankles John . . . Greg.'

'Lee, Nan.'

'Watch my elbows, Lee.'

'What's the suspension like on that road-runner, Nan?' Bill asked.

Clint was slumped in an armchair as if his relatives were vampires collectively sucking the lifeforce from him. At some point, though, he must have summoned sufficient energy to slink away. To hole up in a room in our house with a lock on the door.

'He looks nothing like you,' Mum assured me. 'Does he, Lee?'

149

Melody and Bill's children sat back down on the blue sofa. They were smiling reminders that teenagers are not obliged to be misfits or ruffians. They said things like, 'Doesn't Jacob smell great?' and 'He's lovely, Aunt Lily.' They were really very nice.

Did I say this generation had only produced boys? I clean forgot Melody's April. She looks more like her father than her mother, that's doubtless why. A pale and chunky girl. It's probably just as well.

Greg clipped a Communicam to the base of his mobile and took pictures. John J., needless to say, started making faces like he was trying to poo. Unsuccessfully.

'Tell you what, John,' said Greg. 'Hang on.'

'What?'

He fiddled with the phone. 'Just a sec. There you go, Lily, digital pics already on your computer. I've e-mailed you them.'

Clint reappeared, looking shifty yet refreshed by a bout of self-abuse in our bathroom, and stood next to his father, whom he proceeded to gently shoulder-barge. Greg nudged his son back. Every now and again one of them chuckled. It was simpler than speech, I suppose.

'Can you believe it, Ma?' Lily asked. 'Six grandchildren.'

'Dad never saw one of them,' Mum sighed. 'You'd have liked him, Lily. He was a man and a half, he was. Wasn't he, Lee?'

I realised that Melody must have served up all the tea and cakes without me, or anyone else probably, noticing. It struck me how different she was from Lily. Lily hands dishes round and people stop to say, 'Thank you, darling,' and, 'How delicious.' From Melody people find cups and saucers and plates have appeared in their hands. She's meek. Like Mum, our beloved sister, I had to admit. As if Mum had passed on a self-effacing gene to her only daughter.

*      *      *

Where was I? Oh, yes. Berlin. I wonder whether other people have noticed the dogs there? It's as if dog-leads are against the law; freedom for canines written into the United Germany Constitution. They're everywhere, and they lope at their own speed along the pavements (past dawdling, zombie-like humans, dislocated in another, slo-mo dimension) moving in straight lines on their four legs but with their bodies at a slight diagonal. I've seen them.

One thing affected by the fall of the Wall, not just in Berlin I don't mean but the crumbling of the Warsaw Pact in general, and Russia's dereliction too, has been the quality of prostitutes in Germany. They've reached Amsterdam and Paris as well, presumably. The standard of beauty has shot through the roof; goddesses you would once have hardly dreamed of laying a trembling finger on are now for sale in every shop window and alleyway.

I'm not sure how many men realise what a golden age this is for them. These eras pass us by too easily. It's like the fashion for sports gear a few years back. Suddenly women were walking the streets of England in sporty versions of bras and tights and figure-squeezing knickerbockers. Women's midriffs displayed to the world. Bellies and thighs and even genitalia lovingly described by Lycra. Cotton-clad bottoms wobbling along the pavements of the streets of my country. I remember thinking that heaven was upon us, we'd entered a new Jerusalem, and here we'd stay. But I didn't fully savour the moment, for that is all it was, and the moment passed with the next season in fashion. Clothes shops were full of something else and women's bodies retreated once again behind more demure fabric.

So, a golden age now of dyed-blonde angels with Slavic cheekbones, though not, funnily enough, a golden age for me. When I pay for it, when I have a consumer's choice, I like to fuck a big fat woman. Indeed I do. I've rarely had a problem finding one when the mood has overtaken me: anywhere there was a smattering of whores I didn't need to worry, there'd be at least one large trollop. Which is comforting, isn't it? It doesn't matter how perverse a man's sexual fantasies are, he won't be alone. When Greg first got me hooked up to the net on the home computer I spent a mind-boggling afternoon surfing via links from one website to the next down a ladder of depravity. And what was astonishing, and so reassuring, was that I'd reach a site devoted to the most unlikely and outlandish of proclivities, I don't know, for men who want to dress up as cardinals in gown and gaiters and tie up a Chinese girl. Or to have their balls licked by a toothless poodle. Whatever. I stole into these sites, assuming I must be the first person ever to discover them, only to see a little box that read:

*You are the*
802, 379
*visitor to this site.*

And I, with my own taste in the real world, if hardly weird, for giantesses, was catered for. I was not alone; I found the company I sought (which is curious, isn't it, the idea of ugly whores? Women who can't get other jobs do the one you might have thought them to be uniquely unqualified for.) Except not any more. The poor fat cows are being squeezed out of the market by sheer aphroditic beauty swanning in from the East. No more part-time hausfraus or fat African rumps. No more slatternly, buxom wallops. Customers have got the upper hand and, topsy-turvily, what sneaking men used to have to make do with has become a minority taste, one I share, that's hard to cater for.

I may not be a connoisseur of whores, but I've the highest regard for them. There's too much lust in the world, isn't there? You shudder to think what would happen to it without them. A five-knuckle shuffle is not always enough, men need to be brought off by another's flesh. Orgasm. That's what we're talking about. What it all boils down to. Ejaculation. How incomparably blissful it is.

Why I relish bosomy women, though, I don't know. Neither of my wives, none of my girlfriends, have been unusually large. Lily is long and slender. Is it to make clear for myself a distinction between different kinds of sex? Different orders of relationship? I don't know, really I don't. I like to writhe around with roly-poly women; I like to feel them smother me, absorb me, take me. To ram one from behind, thumping against her buttocks, lashings of gluteus maximus, till my knees turn to jelly.

And as they wobble around, you can almost convince yourself they're enjoying it.

The more flesh the better. An obese girl in an American mall, so fat her own flesh is a medium surrounding her. That she, the real her, has to wade and waddle through with every step. Oh, the fat of such a young woman is luscious, it is the succulence of roast lamb, it is the salivation-making pulp of ripe mango. With a plump girl, a man can grope and poke his way to a delicious, enveloping nirvana.

Myself, I have a disappointing figure. Tall, awkward, not thin – of classical proportions just without the muscle – but rather shapeless. Narrow shoulders, wide hips, scrawny limbs. And now, having entered middle age, a soft paunch; long and puny, yet with loose flab. Naked, I cut an absurd figure, with my thin prick at least proportionate with my frame. I used to suffer a mild form of gymnophobia, the fear of getting undressed in front of other people, of being seen naked, in public changing rooms.

I am plain. Neither ugly nor handsome. Forgettable. I've

tried on occasion the usual methods for improving my visage. Moustaches. Beards. The last, a few years ago, was a bushy one I briefly lurked behind. Lily disliked it. She said kissing me must be like cunnilingus without the fun, and promptly stopped doing so. Instead of going directly to the bathroom and shaving it off, however (which I was anyway considering myself, having hid behind it long enough) I kept the beard a little longer.

*You think I need you to kiss me?* I mean, how can a man be capable of such not merely petty and selfish but clearly self-defeating obstinacy? I know how, and why. Because a man can't allow himself to be pushed around. Because once he lets a woman gain the upper hand, it's over.

Greg grows fuzzy holiday beards. I tried one of those Amish-style ones once. A line of wire around the jawline. The Solzhenitsyn look. I don't know why I tried. It looked ridiculous on the aforementioned and it looked even more ludicrous on me. Off it came.

No more beards for me. I get sharp haircuts now. I go to *Graziani's*, a barbershop in town where cool young men go – the kind of barber I myself never went to as a young man. I'm not even sure they existed in those days, did they? I tell the guy, Number two clippers around the sides, cut square at the back and flat on top. They finish off the sideboards and around the ears with a real razor and warm foam, and they gel the hair, combing it backwards. If I'm going to be middle-aged, I reckon, I want a little dash.

I haven't lacked women. My brother and I had, from our early twenties, wealth and the patina of wealth in our social circle. Chuck a bit of cash around and you get the peripheries, as Greg called them: girls drawn to cars, decent tailoring, and in my case the sheen of pampered flesh. Massages, facials, manicures. Shaves (which reminds me: our father never knew how to shave properly. Bits of grey stubble remained scattered across his chin like a cornfield). Expensive eau-de-colognes. They made me feel good and I also knew what they signified: I soon discovered that in a restaurant or hotel bar I could approach a woman and she'd discern that patina. Whether what attracted her was money – *I'm taken care of here* – or power – *I can relinquish myself* – didn't concern me overmuch.

And because I understood this, I didn't care. I could be relaxed and stand-offish. And this arrogance is the most attractive trait of all. I'd approach a strange woman in a sideways manner, with a throwaway word, and all my signals – voice, look, posture – gave off this unmistakable message: *you want to fuck me? You want to fuck me, you little harlot? Well, I don't know, maybe I'll fuck you. If I think you're worth it.*

Few women resist this invitation, even from a plain, forgettable man like me. Why? Were they weaned too early from their mother's breast, prised loose from the maternal hip? It's sad, pathetic. Don't get me wrong, I love the game, it's given me huge happiness in my life. Or maybe it's just that in casual sex, where we're closest to the animals we once were, and still are, it's obvious that a woman can be persuaded to buckle beneath the man astride her. Once she is vanquished, then she can assert herself. Once he has conquered, a man may submit.

## Stem Canker

Variable-sized black or brown
surface particles on tubers,
easily detached from skin.
Brown lesions may girdle the bases of stems,
causing wilting and rolling of leaves.

# MONDAY 2.30 P.M.

YOU GO round and round, you can go on for ever. As long as you keep your wheels on the ground. As long as you keep with the camber, and work with the centrifugal force; otherwise gravity can turn against you.

I'm not afraid of my brother. He's not my keeper. Greg's not my conscience. I just rather like driving a while longer than usual on a Monday morning. Afternoon, even. I can see why people become chauffeurs. They glide through space, past other people. As long as you stay calm, and let the world slide by, what's the problem?

A lot of fuss about nothing. That's what I just told Simon Wright on the mobile. 'I've thought about it, Simon,' I said. 'I've been giving it some thought, and I don't see how we can allow the random demise of two natives to jeopardise our endeavour.'

Simon still sounded as fazed as he did eight hours ago. I felt like I was talking him down from a high spot. 'If this gets out, we're finished,' he said. 'If the Salesians there find out.'

'Keep calm,' I told him. 'What we have to decide is simply this: whether we stop it getting out, or let it get out but in our version.'

'Oh, John,' he said. 'We never should have done it.'

'Don't say that, Simon,' I said.
'We should have done something else.'

It's the first clinical trial with human beings, after five years working with rodents. If people were told how much AlphaGen had to splash out on lab mice during that time they wouldn't believe it.

The trial has been carried out in stealthy conjunction with an expedition to the Venezuelan rainforest headed by a Professor of Biological Anthropology.

'We couldn't get any more respectable than that,' I reminded Simon. Or responsible, you'd have thought.

Norwalk Virus causes acute gastroenteritis. In developing countries, the rapid and severe diarrhoea is a prominent cause of infant mortality. The virus is spread by contaminated food, and from person to person. It's also known as Traveller's Sickness. Montezuma's revenge. The galloping trots. Lily once told me she's had it on four continents.

'A person hasn't lived, sweetheart, until they've had the runs in an Indian latrine, with pigs snuffling below them—'

'Tell me more, darling,' I interrupted. 'Another time, maybe.'

There's no vaccine available for Norwalk Virus.

Twenty-four supposedly healthy adult volunteers from the same village took part in the trial. They were given cubes of peeled, raw potato: four of them wild-type, twenty a transgenic version, into which Norwalk Virus-copy proteins had been engineered.

Blood and stool were collected. Subjects were observed for evidence of vomiting, cramps, diarrhoea – from the raw potato, not the antigens. Transgenic vaccines, unlike live ones, don't make people sick. It's another aspect to their beauty.

Let's not forget, they were well paid for volunteering, these people. They were given tools, clothing, utensils.

\*  \*  \*

Our baby is teething. He drools. Blood vessels in John Junior's face fill, his cheeks are bright red. He chews his hand, my fingers; biting them with his gums, for relief from the pain. If you peer into his open mouth, you can see the white tooth lurking like a fin beneath the surface of the gum.

Through a combination of the appetite that makes him ever eager to draw edible objects i.e. all objects, towards his mouth, and the attempt to assuage the discomfort of teething, our son often jams his fists, grunting, into his mouth. It is a fine imitation of James Caan (who I imagine got the idea from a baby) as Sonny Corleone in *The Godfather*. Which is confusing for me, since I already suspect when occasionally I glance at our son that those trumpeting breastfed baby's cheeks of his are a joke, that he's stuffed them with cotton wool as an infantile *homage* to Marlon Brando as Don Vito.

I'm now beginning to fear that one of these days I'll come home and find the lights dimmed low, and there he'll be sitting in the shadows like Al Pacino and speaking his first words to Lily: 'Fredo, you're my mother, I love you. But don't ever talk about the family in front of strangers again.'

And that'll be that, really. Next thing you know, Beryl, our cleaning lady, will invite Lily out for a fishing trip in a rubber dinghy on the village pond; the picture cuts to our baby son lying on his mat, while you hear the distant thud of a gun.

But seriously. When he smiles, my son, especially when he's clearly uncomfortable, it's heart-melting. The corporeal condition is such a restriction. Look at his cradle cap, his pulsing fontanelle. See the skin raw in the folds of flesh at his neck, armpit, knee.

I'll have changed his sopping nappy, wiped up his early-morning poo, washed him, massaged his limbs, dressed him. Brought him through to the spare room. Read to him from his little cardboard books – *Peter Rabbit*, *Spot* – that he prefers chewing to perusing. Let him fiddle with his toys. Then he'll have grown tired, and I give him my finger to suck on, and he drifts back into sleep, lying to the right-hand side of me. Then I begin to calculate. To make notes. Sometimes John J. keeps sucking away on my finger for ages, in his sleep. I try to pull it out but suction promptly grips it, and I relent. What a picture: this father lying with knees bent up, a pad on his lap, a biro in his right hand, writing, his left arm laid across his abdomen and the little finger of his left hand in his baby son's mouth.

Our lives are haunted. There's a haunting quality to our lives. We used to think it was something outside us. It is us, of course. The strangeness of the self, the frightening depths of the unknown within us, how much and yet how little we know of what we are made. Most of the time we sidle along, but now and then it happens: we spook ourselves.

It's clearest with new parents – that haunted look, composed of something more than the sum of hollowed eyes, sore heads, movement made awkward from muscles torn by the ridiculous positions in which they've been holding their baby and the quizzical cast to their faces indicating that obvious question: where did I go, my life is that of a drone, subaquatic, so what happened to the real, the authentic, the heretofore me? This haunted look, it comes from even more than any or all of these things, it's just that like little pockets, sacs, of air, they attach themselves and help bring it slow, the submerged moon of the self, to the surface.

Lily is a bohemian. I'm no Round Table, Conservative Club businessman. I don't care what people think of me, as long as they voice their opinions out of earshot; behind my back. I don't need to hear it. The company supports one or two charities in a discreet way. And I'm not one for politics. The mainstay of politics is meetings. You have to enjoy them. The secret of good business is to cut out as many meetings as you can.

I don't mix. I don't seem to need friends outside the family. My first wife, Susan, Jesus, after our divorce I was just relieved not to have to attend any more of our own damn cocktail parties. But Susan, simpering between the canapés, is history. I don't want to waste energy. Our brief marriage was neither good nor bad, there's no need to dwell upon it. I left her behind.

There are, however, occasions when one is forced to socialise with others of the merchant class. And then Lily stands out: a hippy dip between the blow-dried, blue rinse, four-wheel-driving, people-carrying, kids-to-school-run women. I rarely feel fonder of her. I love the New Age nonsense.

Not that Lily accepts a one-way mockery. 'I know a lot of what I do's not rational,' she tells me. 'The tarot's intuitive, I know that. The difference between you people and me is I acknowledge it. You and your brother, you simply don't see how wacky, say, your marketing jargon is. When you talk about, what was it? *The essential role potatoes play in an integral lifestyle experience*? Please. Just because some tough-talking guru in a tailored suit told you that fluffy is the new paradigm.'

Is Lily political? Of course she is. She shops as a radical activist. I can't keep up with who what where she's buying from or boycotting. Fair-trade coffee, cruelty-free shampoo. Organic free-range everything. No factory food, battery hens, child labour. She regards this consumer culture as poisonous, and revels in her consumer power.

163

Lily hates supermarkets. She says the flicker in the fluorescent lighting threatens to bring on her incipient epilepsy.

'You don't have epilepsy,' I told her.

'Exactly,' she said. 'Wake up, sweetheart.'

There used to be a shop in the village. It closed down years ago. Lily cycles around the lanes to local farms and farm shops.

Radical shopping. Yesterday anything from South Africa was banned, or Chile, or France when those nuclear tests were being carried out; today it's China and, I don't doubt, America. America's usually on the proscribed list. Living its life on the open frontier, still, taking potshots of course at the wetbacks trying to swim across the Rio Grande.

It's the same with holidays – where we can or cannot go – except that plans are complicated by Lily's eye for a bargain and a special offer. Like air miles: you fly, you get air miles. The more you fly, the more air miles you get. So the more you fly. So the more air miles you get.

Flying is itself environmentally irresponsible, of course, but wait: if, despite the strip lighting, you shop at *Sainsbury's* you get given free air miles. You don't shop in town, no, you drive round the ring road to the out-of-town supermarket, so you fill up the car, and you get more air miles at the filling station. It doesn't stop. Everyone wants to get you up in a plane, burn hundreds of gallons of fuel, churn through the time zones. A huge plane that swallows you and plunges into the sky. You bank at *NatWest*, you get air miles. Lily buys a new vacuum cleaner, next thing I know we're flying for free.

Last year we took a ridiculous trip.

I remember the first time I flew, accompanying a scientific expedition to Nairobi the long vacation after my second year at Oxford, people applauded after take-off.

This is only, what, 1974. Some scattered palms clapped our relief, the captain, technology. It's already a dead miracle, an event in which the miraculous, the act of 300 tons of plane taking off from the ground with us inside it, has been reduced to zero. And all we're left with is the fear.

Lily had amassed enough air miles to fly around the world a few times. Also she was pregnant, she wanted to fly somewhere before being grounded with a baby. So what does she do? I'd mentioned this chap at the Santa Fe Institute in New Mexico, a physicist who'd turned to money and whose work I'd read about, and Lily decided it'd be fun to build a holiday around my meeting him. She has the love-hate thing with America, of course. So she fixed it up and then she said, 'Why don't I invite your mother?'

'My mother? Sure,' I said. 'And your old uncle . . . the gay Mister Miserable.'

'Sebastian. Great idea,' she said. 'Why not the nephews, too? They'd love to go to the States.'

'They would? To New Mexico? Brilliant,' I laughed. 'What a bunch.'

What a fool, more like. Lily thought I was taking her seriously. She took *me* seriously! Next thing I knew, it was all organised; she'd rounded them up. Dragooned the most incurious, sedentary stay-at-homes among all of our combined blood relations, and there we were climbing into the sky in Economy.

It was a philanthropic gesture. Lily figured it was our last holiday before children, and she wanted to share it. It's the sort of generous gesture that maddens a man even while it makes him fall in love with his wife all over again. To share our last holiday with my widowed mother and her bachelor uncle, to alleviate the awful loneliness of modern old age, yes, but also I believe – in fact I know, because she said so – to give them, to force upon them, a glimpse of sunny post-modern American old age.

Actually, you already have to be in good shape for modern travel: we should have put ourselves onto a fitness regime to prepare for the transatlantic trip. My mother and her uncle anyway. No, the slouching *wunderkids*, too. We had an easy start, at least. I got one of our drivers to ferry us down to Gatwick. That's where the slog starts: you tramp a few miles along tunnels and corridors just to get to your plane. Tall human beings like Lily and myself fold our legs and squeeze into our seats. Then you've got ten hours of thrombosis-inducing immobility, alleviated only by turbulence, wary assessment of your fellow passengers, and the bowel throbs of fear. In Chicago O'Hare, our port of entry, there's a long hike to baggage reclaim, and then the shuttle tram from Terminal Five to Three. Thence a flight to Albuquerque, where you get off the plane and walk across one floor and down an escalator, straight across another floor and down another escalator, and so on and on until you lose count of the floors you've walked directly across and the escalators you've descended because you're thinking that you're trapped in an Escher drawing, no building could be the shape your progress suggests it must be unless it was made from Lego by an autistic child.

The truth is, for every four hours in the air, crossing the troposphere at five hundred mph, you spend five hours plodding through labyrinthine airports.

Most of our fellow passengers were old, spending their sensibly invested savings on travel, broadening their minds by having a look at airports around the world. It struck me how cruel it was, actually, a practical joke; the conspiracy of some coterie of international airport architects (which must be a pretty small club when you think about it, and so quite capable of well-planned sadism) to force these senior citizens to haul their hand-luggage and duty-free for miles around air-conditioned hangars, to tramp the binless-clean, glass-sided corridors, succumbing to stroll fatigue, sitting down on dispersed benches, dropping like flies. Stragglers are picked off by wheelchair-toting, tip-hungry valets, by surly hunch-shouldered golf-cart drivers beeping and flashing the spent, decrepit losers in this game back, doubtless, to a Gate from which a plane will drag them prematurely home.

That's what I thought. And then I realised: I'd fooled myself by focusing on one or two arthritic old stoics limping to a standstill. For they were the minority, the exceptions. Most of the white-haired, wrinkled and eager-eyed travellers were slim and sprightly. They were twice as fit as me.

'Come along, Mum,' I chivvied as she crawled along. 'We'll miss our next connection.'

'Don't take any notice of him,' Lily countered, offering Mum her arm. I'm always thrown by how well they get on, those two. Lily has a mystifying amount of patience for my mother, while Mum feels she's being treated like a proper lady every time Lily opens her mouth. Plus they're always colluding against me.

'He was just like that as a little boy, Lily,' Mum gasped. 'A sly tyrant he was. We won't let him get away with it, will we?'

'Let's ignore him, Ma,' said Lily.

'We'll be forced to leave you behind, Mum,' I warned. 'They'll have to shunt you on after us.'

The fact is, my wife and I do live modestly, but I was lying just now: Lily bought Economy tickets, yes, but I had them quietly upgraded to Business, and there we were, breathing in those recycled germs, those colds and flu, pumping around the cabin, as we flew over the Atlantic with my old ma, the two teenagers and my wife's manic-depressive Uncle Sebastian, who's not just miserable but paranoid with it. He's one of those people who, when he does deign to say something, thinks it'll be so interesting that everyone else will want to listen in. So he talks *sotto voce* and he looks over his shoulder to make sure no one's eavesdropping. He was in a window seat, I'm serious, he did it on the plane. 'I advise you to take the vegetarian in-flight,' he confided, and then he glanced back over his shoulder, out of the window, honestly, at thirty thousand feet. Then he leaned back to me. 'The meat they use is illegal,' Sebastian whispered. 'Animal feed.'

We stayed in Santa Fe, where I met the chap, who explained more about his research into complex systems in phynance: the ways in which he was using computers to model the global flows of currency exchange and commodity futures, searching for pattern and probability. The Institute was established not only to encourage the investigation of complexity but to do so through the open exchange of ideas across disciplines. I found it fascinating, though what it has to do with supplying potatoes is probably not a lot. Selling spuds is simplicity itself! Even if the annual world market is worth a hundred billion dollars, and we ourselves sell almost a quarter of a million tons a year. This chap was sharp, though. Within minutes of me talking, he said, 'I can see where your energy must be directed. At improving potatoes' use in convenience foods. Am I right?'

'Pretty much,' I said. I didn't say anything about Alpha-Gen; it was still early days.

'Tell me about it,' he said. 'Take-out food. Kids are all to go now. In our house, tell them it's time for dinner, they put their coats on.'

'Also,' I said, 'we have to combat competition from alternative carbohydrates.'

'Rice, and pasta. Maize-based products. Imports in general.'

'Imported potato products. Yes, you're right. It's a problem. Kept in check only by a superior increase in our exports.'

It was late summer, and it was hot. We had to drink prodigious amounts of water to replenish that lost through heat and dehydration, which was easy enough to do while we were sweating, but even at night when it was cold you still had to remember to keep glugging back liquid, because of the altitude, six, seven thousand feet.

We were up in high desert country. I imagined the plane that brought us had less touched down in Albuquerque than climbed on to this great plateau. I was reminded that potatoes come from the Andean altiplano, twelve thousand feet above sea level. Wild, knobbly tubers cultivated in Peru, able to grow up there on the snowline, which the Spanish brought to Europe four hundred years ago. Twice as high as northern New Mexico, and here was quite high enough for us to get altitude sickness, me included: dizziness, headaches and a queasy stomach, but without the release of vomiting or diarrhoea.

Every time Clint knocked back another plastic bottle of water, he said, 'It's like clubbing.' Lily had to ask him to please stop dropping the empties at his feet. There was some question as to whether you might be able to drink water from the tap: the answer depended upon whom you asked. Indigenous folk told us, 'Sure. Drunk it all my life.' Most of the people we met, however, were Californians and Texans – Hippies, Artists, Trust Funders – who were making their contribution to urban sprawl into the lovely desert around Santa Fe, and who shook their heads emphatically. 'Oh, no. Drink bottled water. Lots of it. The water table here's full of crap.'

\*    \*    \*

The white-water season hadn't quite finished, so my nephews and I rafted down a stately stretch of the Rio Grande with a guide who said he swept chimneys in the winter. The rafting seemed to exhaust the boys, and they spent the rest of the holiday in slumped postures, in cars or hotel rooms or art galleries, on the verge of sleep. English youth worn out by growing and wanking and the heat.

Clint was clearly locked in that phase when a chap's constantly threatened by a hard-on. That'll spring up on you in public places. The rhythm of a bus, sunlight through a window, never mind an actual girl, the faintest glimpse or scent of whom can bring disaster to a social gathering. Years spent trying to conceal this bulge in your trousers, this massive extrusion you're convinced everyone else can see. Poor kids.

Lily took Mum shopping, which, translated, meant forcing expensive ethnic clothes on to her reluctant body. And urging her to enter the vitamin and mineral culture before it was too late, to make a serious investment in C and E and beta carotene to turn back the premature ageing of, if not my mother's body, then at least her addled brain and nervous system. Then, leaving Mum to recover, Lily tried to work through for herself the complex ethics of haggling with naive Hispanic painters, and with obese Native Americans in the Plaza over their turquoise jewellery.

What Lily's uncle did most of the time I've no idea. He seemed to be mostly somewhere else. 'Cruising,' I told my wife, but she couldn't think of anything else. He really might have found a gay bar in Santa Fe and ensconced himself unsmiling there.

We broke up slogs in and out of the art galleries around Canyon Road with meals in El Farol, or went over to Vanessie and Zia Diner. It was hard to munch through a meal uninterrupted by adjoining tables: our disparate group seemed to constitute a kind of shooting gallery. Inveterate conversationalists felt free to take a potshot at one or other of us. Plus Lily being just visibly pregnant got a few monologues started. One guy, in his sixties, sat straight-spined behind a pot belly in stretch-denim, told us he had four kids and twelve grandkids, and described their various achievements that – he left us in no doubt – reflected every one upon the legacy of his example and genes, before stating most proudly of all, 'I ain't never changed a diaper in my life.'

We looked to his wife to see what she thought of this, but she turned out to be his second or third spouse, childless herself, and apparently as proud of him and his pot belly as he was.

I did a bit of walking on my own, but we attempted one climb all of us together. A stroll up Atalaya Mountain, above Santa Fe, but below the ski area. It didn't look that high and the sign where we parked the car said 2.5 miles to the top. But I confess I should have checked; I was in charge. My ageing mother, my pregnant wife, her old uncle, and two spindly, exhausted lads. We had one small water bottle each and we began to sweat as soon as we started to climb through the pines.

Uncle Sebastian put his head down, stared grimly at the sand and rock path before him and – you have to give it to the old bugger – plodded unfailingly uphill, ignoring sporadic walkers who howdy-ed past us on their way down.

Clint and Lee groaned and argued and gasped, kept stopping out of boredom, so that they then had to jog uphill to catch up or even, with a burst of futile, short-lived energy, find Sebastian up ahead, exhausting themselves afresh, and we'd overtake one or other of them spreadeagled, gasping like a beached fish at the side of the trail.

Lily ambled uphill. It was my mother who was the problem. I didn't realise anyone could walk quite that slowly, without going backwards. It looked like she was putting more effort into *not* making progress than into doing so. It was literally impossible to walk beside her; you could not stop your limbs from opening up this gap between you and her, so that we then had to wait for her up ahead. So although I tried my best to keep us all together in a group – I, the middle-aged Managing Director of a major British potato company, was trotting up and down between people like a tongue-lolling puppy – within half an hour we were strung out along the steepening path.

Dry heat in the thin air has this cell-thinning quality. Up in the high desert. You suck dry air down your throat and into your lungs, you get used to it, and it lifts you. The sweat dries pleasantly on your skin. The sky's blue and huge above the trees and you can believe a peace, a stillness, has settled not just in a small place around you but over the whole earth. You understand why Native Americans came to places like this to take peyote and pray.

An hour and a half passed; Lily and I rose above the luxury adobe homes, finally, and what I took to be the top of Atalaya, glimpsed through the pines, still seemed a long way off. The landscape's on such a larger scale than one's used to in cramped little England that I kept getting space and distance wrong. Then what happened was I was with Lily when we came to a point where the path split: a sign said *Steep Trail* this way, *Easier Trail* that way. We decided to take a break for the lunch of sandwiches and fruit I was carrying in a rucksack, but our dour trailblazer proved to be out of earshot up above us. My mother was way out of sight far below. The boys – I didn't know where they were.

Lily and I decided to climb up the Steep Trail: if Sebastian had taken the Easier fork, we could cut him off.

After a few panting minutes we reached the spot where the Steep and Easier Trails converged, and we waited for everyone else. The first person to appear, though, was a local hiker skimming down the path.

'Have you seen an old chap climbing up ahead?' I asked. 'Seventyish. Medium height. Grim-looking.'

'Yeh, he didn't say hello. Is that the guy? He's stumpin up the mountain, man. Head down.'

It had to be Sebastian. Lily agreed I should scamper up and catch him, while she went back down to where the Steep and Easier Trails diverged, with the rucksack, to meet my dawdling mother. That's where we'd have lunch; that was our rendezvous point. And one or other of us would meet the boys, wherever the hell they were. She'd take the Easier trail down, because that would be the one my mother would take if by remote chance she, coming up, reached the fork below before my wife did going down.

Looking back, it was a perfectly executed fiasco. I climbed, going steadily and disbelievingly faster, till I was practically jogging up the increasingly difficult and steep rocky path, my thighs burning, lungs gasping. I caught up with no one, I saw no one, I was throat-raw for water, but I scrambled up to the top of Atalaya Mountain. There was a fierce, fit-looking American senior citizen who wasn't Sebastian at all. When I addressed him he nodded his head in my general direction. He was wearing chic sleek outdoors gear, in bright colours at stark odds with his demeanour, and I realised that I should have described to the earlier walker Sebastian's white cotton shirt, his threadbare canvas slacks, his scuffed brogues.

But then, with the air in my head, I guess, light-headed, I forgot my responsibilities and looked out across the Rio

Grande valley there. Wide desert beyond. The swooning exhilaration of that enormous, planetary view, earned by one's footsteps and one's own lungs' oxygenated blood. You feel insignificant in that vastness yet so amazed by it it makes you feel as alive as you've ever felt.

Meanwhile. The Steep Trail demanded a brisk clamber, while the Easier Trail wound slowly around a great wide nub of the mountain. Uncle Sebastian had taken the Easier Trail. That was all right, because Lily met him going down, and he turned right around and accompanied her back to the fork, our rendezvous point. My mother, meanwhile, had crept up to that point while my wife was meandering down the interminable Easier Trail, and she, predicting correctly that we would have gone up the Steep Trail, somehow summoned up the energy to attempt it. Ascending, finally, to where the Trails became one again, she sensibly sat down to drink the rest of my water and wait for someone.

No one came. I was at the summit above, Lily and her uncle were now sitting at the lunch place below, and my poor mother sat alone, on what for her was a godforsaken mountain on an alien continent. Eventually she got up and started stumbling back down, on the Easier Trail. And at some point my old mother just walked right off the map. It was a marked path, there were blue diamond signs tacked to tree trunks every ten yards or so, but she didn't notice them, and maybe there was a deer's track, or rabbit's path, I don't know, but Mum stepped off the Easier Trail and wandered into the vast expanse of trees.

I trotted down the path and reached the rendezvous point, and there were Lily and Sebastian, chewing their sandwiches anxiously. Lily and I looked at each other.

'Where can she possibly be?' I asked.

'You came down the Steep Trail, right?' Lily asked. 'Then I just don't know. I can't figure it.'

I did a loop up the Steep Trail and down the Easier one. A few other walkers came up or down and we asked them if they'd seen her, but no one had.

'There's a kid a ways down,' one chap told us. 'Lying by the path. Don't know what the hell he was doing there.'

'Yes, that'll be one of ours,' I said.

'What, you're losing your whole damn family today, feller?'

I didn't need sarcasm from a Yank. 'Yes, thank you for your help.'

'I said, "Are you OK, buddy?" And the kid kinda groaned back. Lying there in the trees.'

There was no sign of my mother. We made our way down, eventually, calmly frantic, as dusk was falling. We found Clint lying beside the path, sound asleep, and roused him. We got back to the car and there was my mother, sitting on a boulder like a little old pixie.

We crowded her. 'How on earth are you? What happened up there? How did you get here?'

She smiled brightly. 'I realised I'd gone off the path, but as long as I kept going downhill I'd be safe.'

She'd come to a house and knocked on the door to ask directions, she told us, and an old guy answered holding a gun. A rifle. He asked what she wanted, pointing the gun at her, and slammed the door in her startled face. My bewildered mother reeled down the road. The man's son, embarrassed by his father's behaviour, drove after her, gave her a bottle of water, and chauffeured her to the walkers' parking spot. Where she waited patiently for the rest of us to join her.

We were so relieved we all forgot about the younger boy, and I would have driven off if Lee hadn't appeared at the last second, having not only reached the top but explored up along the ridge, entered the proscribed water supply area, and seen three deer. 'One of them with the biggest antlers *ever*.'

What's the point? The point of what happened, I think, is this: that we're sovereign individuals. We talk different languages, even when we think we talk the same. It's every man for himself, except for convenience' sake. There's only so much time to help each other up the mountain. At some stage you have to say, 'I'm sorry. I want to reach the top. I'll see you later. I'm going up there now, on my own.'

People get lost on the mountain. The peak awaits the climber. That's the point, I believe.

The other of Lily's interests she was able to indulge in Santa Fe, other than art, was the New Age stuff. It's all there. She saw one woman, Careen was her name. *Internationally Known Intuitive and Spiritual Psychic*. It said on her card she came from *Three Generations of Celtic Healers*. An ancient lineage. It said she did *Cards. Palms. Runes. Aura Reading*. I met Careen. A big cuddly woman, she told me she specialised in multidimensional growth. On her card it said, *The Tiniest Angel Sings the Loudest Song*. I chatted with her before she saw Lily. She was charming. Most of the fruitcakes are.

After dropping Lily off in Pojuaque pueblo, to visit some Native American healer there, I drove on. Up to the Pajarito Plateau. I made a trip to Los Alamos. Why? To get a glimpse of what's happening there. The British laughed at the ludicrous overspending of Reagan's administration on weapons research, but the fact is that that Star Wars investment has seen civil spin-offs in telecommunications, cybernetics, biotechnology.

And, to be honest, I wanted to see and be in the place where the Manhattan Project was enacted. For a man of my age and interests, it's a seminal locus of the twentieth century. Heroic or anti-heroic, it's up there.

Who was it said, *The reasonable man responds to the world. The unreasonable man tries to make the world respond to him?* Which of them inspires progress?

Lily and I argued about it that evening in our hotel room before meeting the others for supper. She'd just come out of the shower. I let slip some jibe at the large and lovely Careen, from her *three generations of Celtic healers*, and my wife jumped.

'Maybe your Oppenheimer could have done with some intuitive healing,' she said. 'Maybe if he'd had some help with his aura he wouldn't have developed an atom bomb. And he wouldn't have had to say . . . What was it he said? *I am death . . .*'

'*I have become Death, the Destroyer of worlds.*'

'How many therapists and healers do you think make nuclear weapons? What damage do they do? Wake up, man.'

I had no answer. Well, that's not true. Of course I had an answer. This was a marital row of a kind we both enjoy. Lily had a white hotel towel around her body, another wrapped her hair.

'Of course they wouldn't develop nuclear weapons,' I agreed. 'No. Nor penicillin. Or automatic washing machines. Or the combustion engines that got us here, for Christ's sake.'

'Good. Good. We don't need to be here.'

Lily's cheeks were inflamed. She had a point. A good one. It was more complicated than either of us admitted, naturally. I dare say, for example, that many Los Alamos employees have their tarots read. Consult their horoscopes. Though not the serious scientists, no. They're more likely to be out in the desert taking peyote with some sorcerer.

But the split is less a theoretical one, between science and superstition, it's about how much we want to affect the world, isn't it? Scientists – and let's not forget the moguls who fund and use them – are the ones who move things forward.

Are we obliged to grow ever more? Is it what we want to do, keep growing to the bitter end, driven only by market forces? Isn't that what this is all about?

Lily and I, meanwhile, argued a little longer, and then we made love before joining the others for dinner. God, I remember how I enjoyed her pregnant body. I loved the feeling of my prick inside her, knowing it was inches from her womb, where the product of my cell and her egg had fused and settled; in which our baby grew. Man, I loved that. Our baby growing inside this woman whose flesh I cherished. It felt so good. I felt like a ruler of worlds.

'Tell me,' the doctor said, 'about the tiredness that sleep does not replenish.'

'It's true,' I said. 'Even when the baby has a good night, and I sleep through his feeds, my wife feeding him beside me. Or nights before I have an important meeting the next day and sleep in the spare room. I wake from seven hours' slumber still tired.'

'Forgive me,' the doctor said, 'but let's not waste time on this. All parents suffer such fatigue. If the sleeplessness doesn't wear you out, the responsibility will. We should move on.'

'I agree,' I told him.

'We've been through everything. I can't find anything wrong. I'm not saying there's nothing wrong. We just can't find it.'

'There's something missing.'

'That's right.'

'No, I mean, what's wrong is there's something missing.'

'What? In you? It's possible.'

'Not in me. In the world there's something missing. I've always felt it, seen it almost. Been frightened of it.'

'Something missing in the world?' The doctor eyed me intently. Studied my face, for what? What symptoms was he looking for?

'And now it's come for me. It comes after those who see it. Or rather, it pulls them towards it.'

'Do you mean God?' The doctor stifled a giggle, I swear. 'Are people still talking about God? The absence where He used to be?'

'No. Yes, of course, God filled an emptiness. But the emptiness was there before God. God filled it for a while, now we're back with it again, I suppose. Some of us.'

'Some of you, yes.'

'God was not the answer.'

'No. Forgive me, but it was, it is, a futile question.'

'Doctor, I don't ask it.'

'Life is there to be lived. Live it.'

'Doctor, I don't ask the question. The question asks itself. It is asked of me.'

'By whom? I mean, you're being tautological.'

'Perhaps. And you, Doctor, are being obtuse. Maybe God is in our genes. God *is* our DNA.'

I'M NOT sure when I became aware of something missing. I think I've always been troubled by it. An emptiness. Inside. Now. Something missing in the future.

Nothing missing in the past, of course not. There never is. I used to sleep with my sister. I never told the analyst that, oh no. Or Greg, or Lily. My little sister made love with me. But in a particular way, in a way she wanted, demanded, and to which I acquiesced.

We discovered this path, Melody discovered her predilection for what we did, I'm sure quite by accident. She was fifteen, I seventeen. We were alone in the trailer one summer afternoon. She came in the kitchen, poured herself a glass of milk, and opened the biscuit tin, to find it empty: I'd just taken the last Penguin bar. She sighed with disappointment, and I said, 'You want this?'

'Oh, yes,' she said.

'Shame,' I said.

'Go on,' she said. 'Give me a bite.' She knew I would. None of us could refuse Melody anything. She was so nicely put together. I'm not saying our sister was physically perfect, but if you wanted to improve her you'd be at a loss as to how to. I tried it once. I studied her, her oval face, almond eyes, lustrous hair, cupid's lips, wondering how

God might have done better. The smallest improvement. I couldn't come up with anything.

'You'll have to get it, then,' I said, holding it above my head. She was taller than average for a girl, but still three inches shorter than me. She jumped up but I swayed it out of her reach. She tried to pull my arms down. We were both laughing.

It just built up, I don't know how, exactly, but she pulled the arm of my hand holding the bar down with both her hands, I pulled her arms apart, and before we knew it we were wrestling, in a way we hadn't for years, since before her puberty when she'd withdrawn from such activity with her brothers. In a way, in fact, we never had.

I fled laughing into the lounge, she pursued me. We had a real tussle. I kept disabling her in some lock or grip, but as soon as I relaxed she went for me again. I was heavier and stronger, of course, but she had stamina. She kept squirming, she kept coming.

At some point I realised how aroused my sister was, that she was turning herself on. At which point I too became excited. We were both sweating and panting. I think it was just luck, our good fortune, that I knew what to do, that I did the right thing, did what she wanted me to do whether she knew it or not: I summoned all my masculine strength and well and truly overpowered her. Got on top of her, held her down. As I began to pull her clothes off she finally relented, a little, enough to let me get them off at all. Her lambswool pullover, white cotton shirt. Unwieldy jeans. White bra and knickers.

She was more ready than I was. I slid into her, into her virgin's juicy vagina. She was already coming, and I soon followed. Watching her in the throes of abandonment struck me to the core of my being.

And after that we did it, occasionally. Always at her bidding. When the others were out. She'd find some excuse to say to me, 'You think you're so tough, huh?' And slap or shove at me. And then we'd get into it. The longer she struggled, the more she enjoyed her ultimate abandonment.

Sometimes she pushed me to the limits of my strength. Her looks had failed to win Melody exemption from her share of crate humping and stall dismantling over the years, the slave labour of a small merchant's children. Melody had muscle. Once, I was tired already when my sister initiated the game and after a short time I'd had enough: I relaxed and said, 'OK, this time you win.'

Instantly she screamed, 'No!' It was frightening. I mean, it wasn't really me, her brother, Melody was screaming at. I don't even think it was her, my sister, who screamed. It was someone else inside her. It was the spirit animal of her libido.

I regathered my strength and fought on and won; Melody suffered her voluptuous surrender, I had my end away.

I believe I have a lot to thank my sister for, in my subsequent relations with women. I'd got off with two or three girls up to then, had awkward, unfulfilling escapades. My sister's gorgeous orgasms dazzled and thrilled me. She made my blood sing. They were wonderful spectacles, and the idea that I had been even a minor agent instrumental in such pleasure empowered me. I hope that I played some similar kind of role for her.

I'm glad to say we never became addicted. We were not obsessive. Weeks, months could go by without her challenging me, surprising me, and I never lost the grateful feeling that what we had was an undeserved bonus, a free gift I didn't have to work for with the usual hard graft of seduction. I accepted each surprising occasion as a stupendous present. But we continued doing it for years.

Be honest, man. We still do. I'm forty-five, my sister's forty-three. I've described how pretty Melody was, when she was in her teens. People would hardly believe it now. For a woman of her age, sure, she's attractive, but her exceptional beauty has been defeated. By bearing children, by living's tension, by the swell and sag of flesh. Me? Oh, I still think she's lovely. I still see that lovely child sinking into her face. And when Melody says, as she did at a cousin's wedding last summer, cornering me in a secluded en-suite bathroom of our brother's house, in whose garden the reception was held, 'Hey, you. You still think you're tough?' I swoon before her stubborn desire, and summon my strength.

What would people think of that? It's true. It really is. I know what they'd think. Greg would kill me, of course, but the rest of them? Those wasters we grew up with? Those sterile nerds in the Oxford labs. 'The lucky bastard!' is what they'd say. Yes. If that didn't make them envious, I can't think what would.

# Skin Spot

Small, round, corky pimples,
often surrounded by dark,
sunken rings.
Eyes may be killed.
Extensive, superficial light-brown lesions on sprouts.

# MONDAY 4 P.M.

I'D FORGOTTEN how much I like cars. Here I am, driving this Merc around the ring road, and I feel as if I've spent the day reacquainting myself with an old friend. I know it's a new model, but even so, it's like an old one's had a face-lift, a spruce-up. Greg likes a Jag. I get Mercs. Walnut dash. Leather upholstery.

I did a bit of in and out, overtaking, just now, to get the feel of this animal and see how she responds to me. I've never wanted an automatic. I can't help thinking automatics are for men who haven't quite figured out where their wife's hot spot hides out. When you get a new car you want to shift up and down, from first through to fifth and back again, stop, ease across into reverse; get to know where everything's located, get to know what's snug and loose, till you know it all and love it like your own wife's gearbox. And then squeeze your foot down on the accelerator. Hear this beauty purr and growl. Feel her pulling us away.

They're going to say I share the blame for the death of two volunteers. Simon Wright panics too easily, he's not used to pressure. You build up a business like mine and Greg's over twenty-five years, you accustom yourself to pressure.

Nineteen of the twenty volunteers who ate transgenic

potato developed an immune response. Generally modest, it's true, but Simon pronounced this a brilliant result. So – with my blessing – he instructed the scientists out there in Amazonia to conduct immediate follow-up research: to challenge all twenty-four volunteers with hefty doses of Norwalk Virus toxin. Yes, all of them, even the control volunteers. Hindsight's a wonderful thing.

I am forty-five years old. I am, as a bright spark at AlphaGen brandishing a research paper promised me on my last birthday, in the middle of my life. We may be in a dark wood, and we may well be lost, but the sun has risen and is illuminating ever greater shafts and shadows and clearings amongst the trees. And we are not looking for a way out. No. We are marching into the heart of the wood, probing its deepest secrets. There lies the light.

John Junior is nineteen weeks old. Our baby is just beginning to develop a sense of humour. He doesn't quite get the peek-a-boo routine yet, me hiding then revealing myself from behind a door or towel. Sure, he may laugh once and, encouraged, I continue, but then he just stares at me, or he turns and looks at something else more interesting. Like a blank wall, for example. You feel stupid. It may be one thing to die the death at the Glasgow Empire, but to flop in front of your own baby? Fortunately, he's developed an appreciation of his father coming gradually closer to him, making slow-motion anticipatory sounds (round and round the garden, like a teddy bear) that end with tickling, or kissing, or best of all blowing raspberries into his fleshy tummy.

John J.'s laugh is a gurgle. It's so pleasant and so pleasing that I wonder whether just as his crying messes up one's brain, frazzling one's thought patterns (Lily and I are the latest parents to discover how difficult it is to drive a car when your baby is crying behind you), so his laughter triggers the release of serotonin or something in my brain: mini-injections of happiness when he laughs.

I made a mistake over what the boy might find humorous the other day, though, which itself was kind of funny. We've had floodlights installed, the sort that come on when movement is detected in a laser beam. To splash a thief with white light. I thought my son would appreciate us creeping along, me holding him and singing the rising notes that anticipate a funny occurrence, then the lights suddenly blinding us. What happened? John J. burst into tears.

My wife came strumping over. 'Did you just do what I think you did?' she demanded, as she grabbed him crying from me. 'Are you completely insane?'

Of all the things I look forward to sharing with my son as he grows up – reading, football, science – it strikes me that comedy is top of the list. The old silents of course, then Laurel and Hardy, The Marx Brothers. I'll stock up on DVDs. Videos of *Fawlty Towers* and *The Young Ones*.

John J. will stare at them stony-faced, I suppose, wondering what it is that's even *meant* to be funny, and feeling somewhat sorry for the old folks. As I did for my father chortling at the frantic antics of Alf Garnett, *Steptoe and Son*. Humour tends to age quicker than anything, doesn't it?

Not as quickly as bad art, which ages in the act of creation, is born stale. Like many wives of successful men, there is in Lily, even as she and we and our budding family reap the material benefits of me and my brother's struggles in the marketplace, a seething frustration and envy. I do my best to soothe it. I tell her she can have or do anything she wants. She doesn't have to bring the baby up full-time – though she can do. Whatever she wants. Nannies, au pairs; child-minders, nurseries. We could afford it, I swear.

There is a part of Lily that's taken on board the modern

injunction that one's first duty is to oneself. But what is this self, exactly? Following the injunction has necessitated the creation, within people's minds, of a new duality. It's as if for Lily there is the one in charge, who makes decisions, lives a life, in the body; one who makes sacrifices for others, sure. She does have personality and will, to some extent, but in reality she is a drone whose only purpose is to protect a more important self, her invisible, sacred self that exists in a more refined and fragile dimension deep within the blunt habitual one.

I can see the future. All over this country there are women whose husbands earn the dough for the family, whose children are growing up and out and away, and who instead of using the expanding time at their disposal for a useful, remunerative contribution to society, find they have the leisure for art. Again, or for the first time; at last.

All over this country, middle-aged women poets, potters, painters (and their middle-aged male partner-patrons). Photographers, sculptors, batik silk-screening designers. What will Lily do when it's her turn? How about *retablos*? Photos, bad snapshots, glued on to driftwood, and painted around and over. That might suit her, it's an example.

Lily's friend, Mira, is a poet. What Mira does is she focuses on some existing area of writing, like gardeners' seed catalogues or travel brochures, collects a load together ('research', according to Lily) and fillets the advertising blurbs for notable arrangements of words. These she sets out on a page in the form more or less of poems. Which she puts her name to.

Mira commits a lot of time and energy to this enterprise, but she couldn't get these poems published. Well, she had one or two appear in magazines, but no publisher wanted to bring out a book of them. So what Mira did was she started framing her poems and hanging them on walls.

In response to my bemusement Lily explained, simply, 'It's conceptual poetry.'

Mira's success was immediate. A couple of years ago our town's one hip art gallery displayed an exhibition of her work. A thin catalogue was printed, hey presto, Mira had her first book published.

'I still don't get it,' I admitted to my wife. To be honest, I couldn't even work out whether the poems said, or were even meant to say, anything about seeds or travel or what have you. 'I mean, she hasn't written a single original word, has she?'

Lily shrugged. 'Wake up, sweetheart,' she advised me. 'We're in the third millennium. Is there anything original left, do you imagine?'

No, I don't think there's anything wrong with it. Not at all. It's not as if artists are superior beings. The opposite, actually: the average painter or novelist has a higher insulin percentage than most people. He or she suffers an increase in random connections between different brain areas. Caused by a gene mutation. Left to itself, evolution will probably select artists out.

No, I think it's wonderful. What better way for people to spend their time? If the husband's strivings in the world of Mammon have earned this leisure, why not use it? Let us each do what we do, and do it on each other's behalf, that's what I say. That's my philosophy. Let the baker bake bread on my behalf. Let the estate agent buy and sell houses so that I don't have to, let a Filipino factory worker solder micro-boards so the rest of us need never think about how our computer works, it just works. Let me and my brother sell spuds for everyone and let the artist explore existence for us all. So I think it's wonderful: let the ladies paint.

Except for one thing. A single objection. *Why impose their work on other people?* That's all. Why do they spend yet more of their husbands' earnings on frames, glass, publicity leaflets, the booking of exhibition space? Why do they issue invitations to their friends rather than their enemies, as well as gullible members of the local media, to a Private View? At which some of the sweeter or wealthier of these friends will pay an exorbitant price for some hideous painting that it would be a kindness to take to the local tip on the way home and put out of its misery. But not only can the friends not do that, they will, having committed this initial error, continue to pay for it, for they'll have to hang the painting at home, won't they? And not in the attic or the bathroom, no, but in pride of place on their living-room wall, for ever. For as long as their friendship lasts.

Why do they do it? Exhibitionism, I guess, a kind of striptease by women without confidence in their bodies, which in my opinion may well be luscious in a child-born way, far more agreeable than their half-baked pieces of pottery or ludicrous drawings.

Men on the whole are less wanton, less shameless. More circumspect, aren't they?

But my wife is a striking woman. Fine bones. Strong bones. Lily's going to look good right through her middle age. Wears her blonde hair cut short. She's a lesbian, actually: she doesn't really *like* men. If we are with another couple or two, for example, at dinner, she invariably addresses and pays attention to the women present. She doesn't on the whole take men that seriously, I don't think. She's at ease in the company of women. When Lily realises that a man is being mildly flirtatious with her you can see her radar go on the blink for a second, she's all at sea, then she'll either make the effort to awkwardly respond or more likely move, turn away.

Lily identifies with other women, and identifies herself as a woman rather than as a human being who happens to be female. She doesn't feel sexually attracted to women, and I suspect this has been an unwitting disappointment to her. She likes sex, and she rarely turns me away, and I sense a resentment of her own attraction to me, as a man; to men as a sub-species.

I like to watch my son attempting to come to terms with his reflection. In the bathroom, whenever I change him, I hold John Junior up in front of the mirror, and introduce him to himself. Sitting at the computer with him on my lap: before switching on, I talk to his reflection in the grey screen. Show him his watery image on the surface of the pond when we take a stroll in the garden. Bring to his attention, his awareness, the ghostly reflection of himself in windows.

The bathroom is actually our godsend, our fall-back position. It seems all parents have one. The place or particular activity in which a grizzling infant may be pacified. A drive around the block to send a sleepless baby off. Or a certain hold, soothing the babe in enveloping arms. For us, it's the bathroom: our boy is happy there. He doesn't mind having his nappy changed anyway, but it's the mirror, surrounded by my wife's make-up bulbs, that entrances him. He is fascinated by his reflection, by the narcissistic boy who stares back at him.

Three in the morning, our son's cheeks are red, his ears ache and his gums hurt from teething; the boy is lost in pain, whining like a grinding machine, and his poor mother who usually soothes him is exhausted. Then I scoop him up and say, 'Hey, mate, let's go see the wee chap who lives in that mirror in our bathroom.'

One glance at that little guy and our son's sobs abate. With clutching breaths he pulls himself together, staring at the baby staring back at him. I move him towards the glass. He reaches out a hand: the other kid reaches out towards him. He touches the glass. Eyes wide. This strange person. I don't know if he gets it yet. I don't know if we ever get it.

'THERE'S NOTHING wrong with you,' the doctor said. 'And yet your symptoms are real. I've considered everything else. There's only one avenue left.'

'Lead me along it,' I told him.

'It's possible,' he said, strangely tentative, 'that this is some kind of allergy.'

I laughed. 'I'm forty-five years old. Don't you think an allergy would have revealed itself by now?' The doctor began to speak, but I cut him off. 'I'm sorry: I don't believe in them. They're not for me. I have the constitution of an ox, I can eat and drink, and breathe the molecules of air, that any man can, keep them down and thrive on their contents. No. It can't be an allergy.'

The doctor frowned at me. 'A hostile response.'

'One must be certain of some things, Doctor. This, for me, is one of them.'

'It's almost as if you were allergic to the very suggestion. Classic symptoms: your face reddened, pulse quickened, perspiration.'

'You're playing,' I said. 'Please. Don't bother.'

'I'm serious,' he said. He paused, looked away, out of the window, then back at me again. 'We're probably talking about something that only recently entered your environment.'

'I can't think what. Do you want me to think about what? Could it be linked to research, is this what you're telling me?'

'No, I wasn't thinking that. Although, funnily enough, I was just reading an article. You may have seen it. They found that people allergic to Brazil nuts could develop an allergic reaction to a genetically engineered soybean that contained one single gene inserted from a Brazil nut.'

'Yes,' I nodded. 'I heard about that. But it's also possible the technology could be used to *cure* those people of their allergy.'

'Oh,' the doctor said softly. 'Right. Yes, maybe. Anyway, apart from that, the fact is, some people are allergic to other people.'

'Really? Are you kidding? To other people in general?'

'To people, to persons, in particular. When we talk of the chemistry between individuals, we're often describing more than we realise.'

I nodded. 'An interesting thought.'

'Let's go through it again: how long have you had these symptoms?'

'Well, as I've told you, I've felt a general physical unease for a year or two. Tragic. It took me until I was forty to feel entirely comfortable in myself, you know, inside my skin.'

'Yes,' the doctor agreed, though he's certainly younger than me. 'An unexpected blessing of middle age.'

'But an ironic one: you accept the body just as it really does begin to go. You leak. In the cold your nose runs. Wet farts escape when you twist. After a piss you continue to dribble. Your body's letting go. A knee burns after tennis. Which reminds me of my favourite joke, Doctor.' I put on a *Pathé News* voice: 'We were short of a doubles player at the club. I asked a chap if he'd like to join us to make up a four, and he said, "I'm a little stiff from badminton."'

The doctor stared blankly at me. As if ready to diagnose the joke.

'I said, "We don't care where you come from. Feel free to join us." '

'Yes?' the doctor prodded.

'Right,' I said. 'So, the contentment was short-lived. Two or three years of this corporeal ease, that was all.'

'And specifically. What brought you to me? When?'

'Well, it was, what, three, four months ago, wasn't it? That the symptoms began in earnest.'

The doctor had been hoping to nudge me at my own speed towards his hunch, but by this point he obviously felt that we'd wasted enough time. 'John,' he said, 'I ask you only to consider this possibility: that you are allergic to your son. That he is the one making you ill.'

I hesitated. 'Are you serious?'

'To a degree, certainly. I may be speaking metaphorically, I'm not sure. But most men when they have a child find themselves gratifyingly anchored in the ocean of life. Or secured in the free flow of time, if you like, finding (or perhaps better, being given) through their child their place in the succession of generations. They are steadied, relieved, placated.'

'Yes. Sure.' The doctor was giving me an if not memorised at least certainly well considered speech.

'Some men, it seems, and one can say especially those with powerful egos, men of power, find having a child has the opposite effect; one naturally exacerbated the later in life it happens. Unlike most people, they were already secure. They saw themselves as great rocky islands in the ocean of faces, of humanity, floating around them. It is having a child that, on the contrary, casts such men adrift. Confronts them with the reality of life's cycle, or procession, and their inescapable imprisonment within it. The child's birth forces an acknowledgement of mortality which, if it is not faced consciously, may erupt in other ways.'

The doctor paused, looked down, held a hand up with forefinger erect and looked back at me. 'In conclusion,' he said, '*most* men gain significance through having a child, while it inflicts upon a *few* a feeling of profound insignificance. You may be one of these.'

My hands trembled. I clasped the arms of the chair, and smiled. 'Thank you, Doctor,' I said. 'That's most interesting.'

M Y HANDS tremble on the wheel. There's Barrow-
bush. Windmill Down. St Hugh's. I shouldn't have
drunk a styrofoam cup of tea at this lay-by last time
around. I don't want to stop again. Is there a bottle or
a bag here I can use? We should keep something in the
car for gridlocks. Having a full bladder while driving's
very specific, isn't it? You can hold an enormous amount.
And when you get out, finally, and unzip by some trees,
you find your prick's shrunk. It grows back to normal
as you pee, what seems like a pint or two of liquid; more
than you ever remember drinking, anyhow.

My brother embraces all forms of male bonding. If some
chap announces that he has to shake hands with the Kaiser,
see a man about a dog, then Greg feels obliged, out of sheer
bonhomie, to accompany him. To stand at an adjoining
urinal, to gaze, head at a slight upward incline, at some
spot on the wall, and piss together. However recently
he's already done so. He's never happier, my brother,
than when jostling for space with a bunch of fellows,
shoulder to shoulder, splashing the porcelain in one of
those unpartitioned, rank urinals with an open gutter; he
never feels more convivial, more fully human.

Me, I'm the opposite. I find it hard to pee in public.

I'm thwarted by the presence of other human beings; other men, at least. I've never had that problem with women, with lovers. That terrible intimacy, isn't it? Did other people wonder about that when they were children? I did: do couples go to the bathroom together? A man and a woman? I could imagine sex from the moment I gained an inkling of what it entailed, but doing the business with her in the same bathroom? Her, with me there? Disgusting.

Since growing up, I rather like it. Pissing, certainly. There's something enduringly girlish about one's wife peeing. On a long drive, for example. You stop in the middle of nowhere; I step to the verge, and while I unzip my flies and empty my bladder of milky piss I watch Lily unpeel her leggings and knickers as she squats. When I've finished myself I sidle over and watch her piddle stream along the ground from between her feet. Why is that so appealing? I don't know. I'm sure other people know more about these things than I do.

Occasionally Lily will let me lie beneath her. She claims it doesn't turn her on, though I don't see how that's possible. Says she only does it for me. When we bought the house, in the trees beyond the lawn, I can feel the moss below me, she squatted and peed on my face.

I've got so much to think about, I almost forgot about what happened at the weekend. There are four concerts annually, organised by our choirmaster, and Saturday night saw the first of the year. He'd invited Bjorn Lungstrom, the Norwegian pianist, to come and play Chopin, Debussy and Ravel in our village church. All two hundred and sixty tickets were sold out in advance, proceeds going towards famine relief. And Lily and I offered the use of our house and garden for interval refreshments.

It's become a part of this modern tradition that the intervals are catered for as if the concerts take place in high summer: a glass of white wine, strawberries and cream, consumed standing on someone's lawn. Although the house has to be made ready or a marquee erected and standing by, members of the church claim that all but one or two of the twenty-odd concerts thus far have taken place on what turned out to be days of unseasonably temperate weather for spring or autumn, evenings on which it was a delight to be outside.

Who were we to argue? I ordered thirty boxes of Chablis, orange and apple juice, two hundred punnets of strawberries from Israel and tubs of whipped cream – all, according to Lily's instruction, organic. All this we paid for, as part of the hosts' customary contribution – a sort of toll for membership of the village establishment.

I left it to my wife to hire caterers, but she insisted on recruiting the nephews and their friends.

'Clint and Lee want to do it,' Lily said. 'Earn themselves some money. And it'll do them good to do a bit of work for a change. Look at them: their laziness is crippling them.'

'Honey,' I said, 'do you think that's wise? You know how oafish our nephews are, and their mates are doubtless worse. People won't want to have their drinks spilled by ruffians who look like they're about to mug them; they want to be served by pretty girls in black skirts and little white pinafores. I don't blame them.'

'Oh, wake up, man,' she said. 'We're in the twenty-first century now. We did make it, you know. You're given an opportunity to combat stereotypes, both the concert-goers' and the boys', and all you can do is moan about it.'

I didn't argue, though I knew I was right. People depend on protocol. The more casually we dress, so workers in the service industry get smarter. You go to a cocktail party, you go to the opera, and millionaires are dressed for the weekend. While minimum-wage waiters and waitresses serve you in neatly pressed white shirts, trousers with creases in them, leather shoes that shine.

Anyway, the day came and what do you know? Easter's late this year but still, it was the mildest day of the year so far; almost balmy, it could have been June. The sun rose in a blue sky and gently warmed the morning. I hired the muscle of some men from work to collect rented trestle tables, chairs for the infirm, wine glasses, cups and saucers, cutlery. The food and drink was delivered: the fruit supplier, an old competitor when we were still small traders called Bob Canman, came in person and found me overseeing Richard's gardening gang sprucing up the lawn and flowerbeds.

'Listen,' Bob said, as we reached the back door where he'd parked. 'I'm awful sorry, John, but there's been a mistake. I ordered them direct from Tel Aviv myself.'

'What mistake?'

'They're not organic.'

'Tell me you're joking.'

'They're beautiful strawberries, though. Here, taste one.'

I ran it under the tap and put it in my mouth. It was soft and succulent and sweet, it melted in the saliva on my tongue. It gave one that sensation rarely known: that you're tasting fruit about five seconds past its peak, its zenith, of ripeness. It was the most perfect strawberry I ever ate. So was the next.

'What I've done,' Bob said, 'is I've put them into boxes marked Organic. But at the same time I'm telling you.' He looked at me with the anxious expression of a man without power who's taken the initiative.

I took a twenty from my wallet, nodded towards the figure sat behind the wheel of Bob's van. 'You did the right thing,' I said, slipping the note into his hand. 'Treat yourself and the lad there to a pint on the way home.'

\* \* \*

Three of Clint's pals helped unload the boxes of strawberries from the van to our scullery. Each of them wore his hair identically sculpted with gel and plastered close to his skull, in a style that in barbers' sign language declared, HERE IS A TEENAGE CRIMINAL. They sniggered to each other, though they found it impossible to speak or even look at me; when I spoke to them they could only look away, at some unspecific spot, with an expression of resentment at my having addressed them.

'Wash the strawberries in the sink at the back of the garage there, and put a helping into each of these bowls,' I said. 'About this many,' I showed them. There were four hundred bowls. 'And put dollops of cream on all but a few while the first half of the concert's in progress.'

I left those lads to it and took Lee and his best mate with me to plant stakes along the verge from the church to our entrance. Being the Old Rectory, this is not far; we're next door, in fact, though owing to the layout of the churchyard and our garden and the curve of the lane, it's a two hundred yard walk. There used to be access across the lawn and through a small gate into the graveyard, for the Rectors of past times, but what with the dead buried in the new cemetery out on the edge of the village and atheistic occupants before us, this gateway has grown over with disuse. And our new perimeter fence has now stoppered it for good. So this pair of boys helped me skewer four stakes with cardboard signs tacked to them promising:

**Refreshments This Way**  →

They took turns to hold the posts steady while I thumped the tops with a sledgehammer: neither of them could quite raise the hammer with ease and I certainly wasn't going to trust them swinging it. I was reminded how weak a boy is, how enervated by adolescence, until all of a sudden the testosterone kicks in, muscles are defined, and one feels oneself to be strong. A young man, at last. And after that you think you'll get ever stronger, this is something you assume, and you will for a while, for ten, twenty years. Until one day you'll go to lift a familiar weight – a sack of spuds, say – and find it's a heave, a strain to accomplish. In middle age you experience again the weediness of puberty.

I bathed and changed into black trousers, anemone-blue silk shirt and jacket and was looking out of our bedroom window at the garden when my wife came up from behind and hugged me. 'It looks great,' she said, though I could tell she was leaning her head against my back, and probably had her eyes closed, too. 'Everything's ready. Beryl's here.'

Our cleaning lady was going to supervise the catering operation. Lily wasn't quite naive enough to leave our nephews and their fellows entirely in charge of themselves.

'How's our boy?' I asked.

'I just fed Jacob,' she said. 'He's gone to sleep. Sonia's here to keep an eye on him.'

'You're happy to leave him?' I asked. 'The first time.'

'I'll sit in a pew by the door,' she said. 'I've got your bleeper. It'll be fine. I don't want to miss it, especially the Chopin.'

'I know. Well, let's stroll over.'

'Hey,' she said.

'What?'

'I'm glad you're not wearing a tie.'

I hadn't thought about it. 'You don't want me to, do you?'

'Of course not.'

'I'm OK like this?'

'Yes,' she said.

'You're happy I'm not in cords and tweed? You know, I said I didn't want to go rural.'

Lily laughed, shaking her head.

'You look stunning,' I told her. She was wearing her Nicole Farhi black slacks, a charcoal cardigan, and she'd painted her face. My wife does the abracadabra women do, this metamorphosis into painted elegance. Lily smiled graciously at my compliment. She kissed me, lightly, so as not to disturb her lipstick.

'You know I love you,' she said. I think she maybe even believed it.

'We're doing OK, aren't we?' I said.

We walked hand in hand round to the church. People greeted us, I was surprised at how many folk we've got to know here already. The choirmaster was at the door, presiding in a regal way, and why not? He deserves it. The Rice-Wallingtons were there, the old moneys in the village, decrepit aristocrats: they both look worn out by the effort of a lifetime spent affecting aloofness. Jeff Flyme, who calls himself a farmer, though I can't see him on a tractor, somehow, with his young partner, his catamite really, Shay, a chap with whom my wife falls into instantly profound conversations whenever she sees him.

The Rector, Justin, caught my eye, and winked. I was surprised to see him – and his wink included acknowledgement of this – because I know music doesn't do much for him, and this little parish is one of six he covers, so he was under no obligation to come. He wasn't wearing a tie, either, never mind a dog-collar. I like Justin. He's barely thirty, and he seems to be one of a generation of whom even the clerics seem to feel no need to profess faith in an outmoded religion. But, Justin told me, the church still provides not only a social function, but also a legitimate forum to discuss ethical issues; it's just that today priests need no longer justify opinion with, 'Jesus tells us this,' or 'According to scripture.'

Last time we met, Justin collared me and said, 'Tell me, what is it with this GM thing?'

I blanched. 'What do you know about it?' I asked him.

'Only what I read,' he said. 'But you're in the food business, aren't you? These suicide seeds. This terminator gene. I mean, is it really going to feed the starving, or what do you think?'

Of course there were many strangers amongst the audience. As they filled the pews I sat down near the front next to Jo Bingle, Lily's best new friend in the village, a young spinster who has her own shop in town selling funky kitchen equipment, and a cottage along the lane here with a stable and paddocks; she'd offered a field for tonight's car parking. Jo asked where Lily was and I nodded over my shoulder.

'By the door, just in case,' I told her. 'The baby. She said to me to sit here and say hello. How are the horses?'

'Pony. Fine.'

'You looking forward to this?'

'Of course. It's the occasion as much as the music, isn't it?'

'I guess,' I agreed. 'The Chopin should be good.'

It was almost seven-thirty. I closed my eyes, let my mind listen to the sing-song cacophony and the peculiar hushed bustle of secular concert-goers in a country church. I inhaled the scent that Jo was wearing, concentrated my attention towards the barely discernible contact of our beclothed thighs – my trousers, her skirt and glossy tights – and idly wondered whether we'll ever have sex together. Not vividly enough to encumber myself with a substantial hard-on; just, you know, with that semeny feeling flowing to and fro in my prick.

Then there was a sinking towards silence, as people's voices drained away: I opened my eyes, to see the choir-master mounting the chancel step. After a short introduction he gave us Bjorn Lungstrom, who entered from the vestry to enthusiastic applause. Justin, I fancied, must have envied him this reception.

Lungstrom played our Bechstein beautifully, so far as I could tell. I mean, I'm no judge. I had a good view and, to be honest, my appreciation was as much of his athletic as his musical achievement. His feet drew my attention: stepping on and off the pedals with what looked like involuntary, reflex movements. Self-obsessed little feet. Their hiccuping dance seemed to bear scant relation to the music.

Lungstrom started with a piano transcription of Mussorgsky's *Night on the Bare Mountain*. I'd read the programme notes, I knew the quadruple *forte* and daring harmonic figures were inspired by hellish Russian fairy tales. But what it made me think of were silent movies – whose piano accompaniments were of course prompted by just such nineteenth-century music as this. As if, due to my ignorance, Mussorgsky ripped off the music he inspired, when I closed my eyes I saw blurry black and white characters running around and over-acting furiously. Keystone Cops, *The Perils of Pauline*.

That's what I do in concerts. I let the music lead me into whatever daydreaming narratives it will, conjure whatever images appear. I envy people who can concentrate on the music itself. Sometimes the music virtually evaporates from my awareness altogether and does no more than seal me off within an unrelated stream of thought. So it was after the Mussorgsky. Bjorn Lungstrom began playing Schumann, and my mind drifted.

When Lungstrom finished the first half of the programme

I glanced round and saw, through a storm of applauding people, Lily slip out. Feeling no need to hurry myself, I strolled home in the midst of the procession, as if I too needed to follow signs on the stakes I myself had embedded. Delegation is one of the first rules of leadership. Once an event is organised, you sit back and relax; you don't fret. Worry helps no one. Confidence reassures.

To my surprise, a light rain had begun falling. Scattered individuals put up umbrellas, or pulled a small square of transparent plastic from a pocket and kept unfolding it until they had one of those superlite macs to put over their clothes; I'm always impressed by people who are prepared for unexpected weather. One or two ladies held programmes above their hairdos. Most of us, however, put up with damp head and shoulders as we ambled in the warm evening around to my house. Now that we were walking, I was struck as I had not been in the church by how many of the audience were elderly, stuttering along leaning on walking sticks or companions' arms.

Everything was under control in the garden. My wife had had the bright idea of persuading the lads to adopt some kind of uniform by suggesting they wear their Manchester United replica shirts. There were two or three dissenters who vowed they wouldn't be seen dead in strawberry-coloured red, so they wore their own teams' colours. The boys were all impeccably polite. I was amazed to see this Chelsea hooligan help a decrepit gentleman to a seat and that Newcastle lout guide ladies in the direction of our lavatories, as well as a phalanx of Red Devils doling out the booze and the fruit efficiently. You could tell it went through everyone's mind: *What a novelty, these pleasant yobs.* You have to hand it to Lily.

Spotting Jeff Flyme smoking by a rose bed, I grabbed a glass of wine and went and cadged a fag off him. We chatted, but I let Jeff's words float by and savoured instead the wine and smoke succeeding each other on my palate; the alcohol and the nicotine sneaking into my bloodstream, along the arteries, around my brain, while two hundred and fifty guests stood on our lawn, partaking of our hospitality, eating deliciously ripe strawberries with castor sugar and whipped cream. The rain ceased altogether, and the sky cleared.

Having successfully breastfed our boy upstairs, Lily rejoined me, and we returned to the church. Again the slow shuffle along the lane, like a column of refugees seeking sanctuary.

Bjorn Lungstrom (having, it was whispered, spent the interval meditating in the vestry) began the second half of the programme with Chopin's Piano Sonata No 3 in B Minor, op 58. 'The first great B Minor Sonata of the Romantic era,' Lily had told me earlier, 'but also Chopin's last great work.'

'Really?' I asked.

'The defining monument of the Romantic imagination.'

I tried to concentrate. It was pretty wonderful. Like that surprise you get at *Hamlet* or *Macbeth* as you're reminded how many epigrams in current usage come from Shakespeare: whatever thematic integrity Chopin might achieve, almost every phrase conjured a new, exemplary stream of gorgeous notes.

My attention was distracted when I glanced at the programme and saw that Chopin died at thirty-nine. Six years younger than me – and, according to my wife, he'd completed his best work five years earlier than that. All of them – Mozart, Chopin, Schubert – died younger than I am now. Schumann had already gone insane.

I watched Lungstrom play: I could just see his hands from where I was sitting. He wasn't reading the music, no, he knew it by heart and he was inside this sonata of

208

Chopin's. He had the courage of a swimmer who plunges into a water-filled quarry from a steep rock face, knowing that to get out again he's got to swim right across to the other side. So Lungstrom in striking the first note dived into the music, and there was no turning back: he was trapped inside the sonata and the only escape was to play his way out of it. The music possessed Lungstrom. And it possessed us, too, but Lungstrom would free us all. If only he could remember the notes and play them in the right way, the most expressive, the most liberating. It looked to me like he could, this young Norwegian. He was magnificent. The more I watched him, the more handsome he seemed to be.

Which is something I've noticed before: music makes musicians beautiful.

At this point in my musings – still in the first movement of the sonata – I became aware of a noise behind me, the sound of human movement. A minute later, the same; and then again. I glanced around and saw Mrs Grane, the church-organist, walking out. Then, over here, some-one coughed. Soon, over there, another person stirred. A moment later a chap sitting in the pew in front of me lurched forwards and sideways and propelled himself to the side aisle and out: he was bent double, discreet as pos-sible, true, but still it seemed extraordinarily rude. Surely Lungstrom wasn't that bad? Maybe he was. Or maybe the aficionados amongst us had been spoiled by recordings, by listening to too much perfection, to the Ashkenazys and Brendels in a favourite armchair with speakers situated just acoustically so. In clean, digital surround sound.

I don't know enough about music. Not nearly enough. Maybe Lungstrom was murdering Chopin's Third Piano Sonata, he was committing some cardinal sin that the true connoisseurs amongst us recognised. I didn't know. We've got used to being a placid, passive audience, haven't we?

In the days of early modernism people cared enough about art to throw insults and objects at musicians; members of Stravinsky's orchestra hid behind their cellos and chairs. Perhaps a revival was taking place right here, right now, music lovers stalking out of our village church in high dudgeon. The rest of us philistines were lapping up what was actually an insane affront from this Nordic nutcase engrossed in his playing a few yards in front of me. Maybe he wasn't even playing Chopin any more! Maybe he'd gone off into his own lunatic doodles along the keyboard!

Lungstrom was seated at the piano side on to us, and so possibly unaware of what was happening in his audience. But it continued: the piano notes interspersed, interrupted, by people pushing their way out of crowded pews, by urgent footsteps across the stone floor. Did Lungstrom realise people were leaving? Maybe he did, but it didn't matter, he couldn't stop. He knew he had to carry on playing that piece of music note by perfect note in order to release us all from that church. If people seemed to be leaving, that could only be an illusion, one devilishly created, precisely to tempt him to stop.

Next thing I knew, Jo beside me put a hand over her mouth. I looked at her and saw her eyes, above the horizontal fingers, were horrified. Like a silent-movie heroine. Had Lungstrom just played some infernal note? She was sat at the end of our pew, beside the centre aisle. She sprang out of her seat, and I watched her scuttle down the aisle and out of the door, which was no longer being opened and closed between individual exits: too many people were leaving; from all corners of the church they were rushing out. Lily got up as Jo reached the door, and left with her.

It struck me suddenly that perhaps there was something wrong in the atmosphere of the church, a gas leak or some such. I sniffed the air, but detected nothing.

Lungstrom was still playing, still seemingly unaware of the anarchy erupting in his steadily depleting audience. He did stop, but only to take a deep breath, before embarking upon the second movement, the *Scherzo*. His fingers fluttered across the keys.

At this point I decided to act. The capacity for leadership involves a readiness to take command of a situation, whatever it is. One recognises that leadership is required. I got up and walked, straight-backed, down the aisle. Even during those few seconds another two or three people rose from various pews and, still attempting to do so unobtrusively, bent double and fled.

Outside, dusk had fallen. What is called in cinema, I believe, the magic hour was drawing towards its end: that uncanny light after the sun has gone down, but before darkness settles. I saw Lily in the middle of the graveyard, and I hurried over. She was kneeling beside Jo, with a soothing hand on her back and words in her ear. Jo was bent forward and vomiting the reddened contents of her stomach on to the ground.

I looked around. Mrs Rice-Wallington tottered out of the church, clutching her guts, stumbled across the grass, reached a gravestone and collapsed behind it. Justin, the Rector, came dashing out of the porch, unbuckling his trouser belt as he ran. When he had, evidently, to stop, he stopped, pulled his trousers down and squatted, and gave himself over to the diarrhoea that poured from his arse. Old Major Rice-Wallington followed his wife outside, reached a clear piece of grass, lay down, curled up on his side, and with a sad groan both threw up from one end and let the seat of his white flannel trousers fill at the other.

Strangers followed them. I wanted to help but I hardly knew where to start, beyond calling for an ambulance on my mobile. Having done so, I stood and stared. Some people managed to crawl behind gravestones to shit or spew with some semblance of privacy, but most, way beyond caring, were content to reach an open space, which became ever harder to do for those still rushing out of the church. A bottleneck built up along the path.

A pretty young girl, seven or eight years old, took one neat step to the side of the path, pulled down her knickers and quickly crouched, her skirt falling discreetly around her. Shay, Jeff Flyme's partner, floated past – almost over – other people like a sleepwalker, then was promptly jerked sideways like a puppet and let loose a stream of red projectile vomit over the prone, semi-naked body of a large, elderly lady. I registered that the body was Mrs Grane's, the organist, at about the same nanosecond it struck me that it was the strawberries. Arsenic, as an illegal preservative, is still sprayed, in some parts of the world, by unscrupulous bandit growers. On fruit delivered by one spiv of a supplier called Bob Canman. On the strawberries that those lazy, insolent, useless little bastards had, once my back was turned, not bothered to wash.

The worst thing was the sound: the involuntary groans of people as they began to puke. Yet in the background, one could still hear Bjorn Lungstrom's piano, Chopin issuing from the church. He was into the *Largo* now. I was able for a moment, through an instantaneous act of will, to shut out the sound of groaning and vomiting and, I swear, increase the volume of the Chopin. Good God, it's splendid music.

The choirmaster emerged: he stumbled towards a grave with a stone bed above it filled with chips of blue quartz or crystal. He knelt as if to pray there and, for a few moments, looked as if he was sobbing – until you realised he was retching, before he brought up the red-stained vomit on to the blue grave. It seemed like a terrible sacrilege was being committed; but whether to the dead or to the living, I wasn't sure.

'For Christ's sake,' a voice jarred in my head. I turned. It was Lily. 'Are you going to help, or what?'

I must have gaped at her. She'd grasped Jo's shoulders, was helping her stagger along the path out of the churchyard.

'Run to the house. Get everyone there to drop what they're doing. Find blankets, bring them here. Have hot water and flannels and towels ready over there.'

I gazed back at the scene. I just needed one more second of the spectacle before me. One more minute to discern its meaning. It was so beautiful, somehow. This virulent disgorgement in a country churchyard. Sea-sick, strawberry-sick, music-sick Christians, feeding the fishes. Manuring the graves of our ancestors.

Resurrection.

'Go!' Lily said.

I ran.


Face it, man, you're not going to work today, are you? The afternoon rush hour's building up. It'll be getting dark soon.

Where's that phone? Simon, I have an idea.

# Black Dot

Dark brownish-grey surface blemish
of tubers.
Sclerotic dots give a sooty
appearance, often developing a
silver sheen in store.
Occasionally stems, roots and
stolons affected, leading to
wilt,
wilt,
wilting.

# WEDNESDAY 8 A.M.

Y OU HAVE to think laterally, that's what you have to
   do. I told Simon, I said, 'Simon, these villagers are
fierce warriors, everyone knows that. They're rain forest
hooligans. I wouldn't be surprised if it turned out our
volunteers were killed by enemies from another tribe.
What do you think?'

Mobiles have their own cramped acoustic, their own
silence, in which you could hear Simon's brain swooning.
'John, I'm on to it,' he said, and cut me off.

And now it's good to get back in the car: we've spoken
on the phone a great deal these two days since, but now
I'm driving to Cambridge. On to the M6, then the A14
all the way. Simon says a battle took place yesterday. The
scientists were unhurt.

He says we'll start a new trial, in this country, with full
medical supervision.

'Good,' I said. 'Let's keep calm. There's no need to begin
tomorrow.'

We're going to discuss it when I get there.

Lily was mortified after the concert last weekend. I promised her we'd sue Bob Canman. We'll sue the Israelis. Hell,
we can sue Clint and his cohorts: we'll take those kids for

every penny they've got. Lily still said she didn't know how she was going to be able to show her face in the village again. But then in the morning she announced that she was going to go to church, which shows the kind of spunky character she is. So after I'd made her breakfast, she took John J. and went.

I was worried she'd come back crushed, ignored by idiots unfit to act as her prayer stool. In which case we'd be leaving this village. And who'd give a damn? We're OK. We're a family, and we'd just drive out of here.

Instead she returned buoyant, told me what so and so said, and such and such was wearing, and what Justin, looking somewhat drained and unsteady in the pulpit, preached in his sermon.

It's spring. Smells rise from the earth. All along the bank of the ring road leading to the roundabout daffodils have bloomed. Old men cycle through town in slow motion. Yesterday was positively warm, layers of winter clothes were divested and it was as if overnight there'd been a female influx, a fresh population of women imported into our town.

'We've been taken over by Amazons,' Greg declared. 'They're everywhere.'

'Girls are bigger than they were in our day,' I agreed.

'Our day?' he said. '*Your* day, you old fart.'

'What about the boys?' I asked him.

'What? You see men?'

'You don't see men?'

'No,' he said. 'Not really.'

I considered this. 'Neither do I,' I told him. 'Except the old ones.'

'They come out with the spring, too,' my brother laughed. 'Old men and young women.'

\*     \*     \*

I told Greg everything, yesterday lunchtime. I dragged him to a pub. He listened. I said, 'Trust me, brother.'

A memory keeps recurring. Our Uncle Ray. My mother's brother. He was detached from our family. An oddball, thoughtful, a self-taught scholar; he'd moved from town to country, made a living fashioning cast-iron beds, was it? No, bannisters. Railings. With decorative swirls and knobs and flourishes. I forget exactly. He had a workshop.

Our uncle had no family of his own. My mother mentioned a ladyfriend, but I never met her. I suspect Mum made her up to reassure herself, to make her brother seem less strange to her.

Dad smiled indulgently whenever his brother-in-law was mentioned. 'He's made nothing of his life,' he'd say good-naturedly. 'And why should he?'

'He gets by,' Mum would say.

'Why not? That's all he needs to, he's a bachelor.'

'His ladyfriend has her own means.' As if no woman who did would marry.

The fact was our uncle was a loner. He'd cut himself loose. But for a time, a period of less than a year when I was ten or eleven, I visited him. I'd be packed off on the bus and be carried the twenty-odd miles into the country to stay for the weekend.

This memory keeps recurring: the first time I went on a ramble with my uncle. On the Sunday morning he fried a breakfast and then went and sat down in his favourite chair and picked up a book, as if I wasn't there. He'd forgotten I was, or saw no reason to explain the due order of events in his house. So I sat down and read, too. I was a bit of a reader, did I say that already? And then at some point, when I was engrossed in whatever I was reading, I was snapped out of it with the slap of his book down and his abrupt exclamation, as if he'd suddenly noticed I was there: 'Boy! Let's us go ramble.'

This memory recurs. We walked a while, side by side when our path ahead was apparent, me following otherwise. Saying nothing. I sank into my own thoughts. Into the book I'd been reading. I don't know, *Rogue Male*, perhaps; *Kidnapped*. Some adventure. Or off on one of my own boy's fantasies. Occasionally looking around, seeing nothing other than hazards such as nettles and brambles, sinking back. We – me and my family – lived in the town, where every movement signified something human, or mechanical, that might be relevant to one's survival, or at least entertainment. This landscape we walked through was uniform: wherever you looked, either trees or fields.

My uncle's first words on our ramble were, 'That's far enough, I reckon. Better get back for lunch, boy.' And then this question: 'What did you see?'

I was flummoxed. I remember my feelings acutely: embarrassment, resentment, shame. I'd been wrong-footed. As if I'd walked into an exam and been faced with a paper for which I was unprepared in a subject I'd not even studied. Yet there was no mistake, it was certainly my fault, because my uncle's question clearly implied that there were things I could have seen, but had failed to. I understood this to be true. I mumbled some evasion.

On the walk back, the ramble home, Uncle Ray brought to my attention landmarks we passed. He named trees, birds, crops growing in fields. He pointed out edible plants, and the habitats of animals, upon which a resourceful man could survive. I remember it with the peculiar acuity of a dream because that is how I experienced it. I drank in every sight, the world broken down, broken open, revealing its secrets as my uncle beckoned them with his words. Science before it interferes.

'What you see, you own,' he said. 'It's yours. All yours.'

For a year or so I became an avid nature lover, my pre-pubescent boy's hungry mind consuming lists of flora and fauna. Took that bus whenever I could, weekends and school holidays. In the winter I slept in his bed. He taught me to cook. But mostly I wandered. I saw. I owned.

'What do you *do* out there?' Greg asked me.

'I go rambling,' I told him, and I didn't want to explain.

But I grew up, girls began to turn my head, I played football. I stopped going to see my bachelor uncle in the country. I laid my plans. Uncle Ray died. But his words that first day: 'What did you see?' The memory keeps recurring.

It may be that growth only comes, or came, with fear of death. That it was only when human beings became uneasy with their place in the cycle of life and death that they developed technology in the first instance.

Mortality comes ever more to mind in middle age, naturally. My family background provides no compass for approaching death. Our grandparents had already joined the twentieth-century drift from religion: my parents may have exhibited still the proud incuriosity of that part of the English working class they came from, but they'd bravely shrugged off the dumb faith that used to go with it. So I possess no liturgy learned by rote, no ingrained dogma, with which to deal with death.

I study my son. I see no evidence of behaviour that may suggest his having lived before, see only his slowly forming brain. As for myself in him, there's consolation in that, of course. I should hope so. More than anyone has ever had before me. Well, we want some payback, right?

Our son is so robust. At nineteen weeks old so big and fat and cherubic, that I have no fears about his health. I really don't worry at all that John Junior might have something seriously wrong. He's given me no cause to. Tiny symptoms

– rashes, coughs – that Lily spots and anxiously alerts me to, I shrug off. 'It's nothing,' I say, and I mean it. And it is nothing, it goes away.

I've only one worry. Not that he will be sickly, but that he will die. Cot death, stopped breathing in the night. A monstrous fit seizing his healthy body. Ridiculous.

The fact is, now that he's made it this far, an infant today is likely to live long. A hundred and fifty years, according to one of the AlphaGen chaps. As long as I make some money for John J. to inherit and hang on to, so that he can afford the necessary treatment along the way. Virtually immortal, says the biologist.

AlphaGen and ourselves agreed a couple of months ago to proceed upon the assumption that the Norwalk Virus clinical trials would be successful, and planned how best to work together on bulking up the materials AlphaGen had produced in laboratory tissue culture, for larger-scale testing. They already have almost enough seed to put out a whole field of potatoes.

Such planting will not be possible in this country for years. Even in the States, government permission to grow the crop outdoors is not quite forthcoming. We could work in glasshouses there, but field trials are essential as soon as possible. I've earmarked an out-of-the-way spot over in the Marches. There's a farmer grows potatoes for us in a remote valley. No lanes, no footpaths, pass close by. I'm confident it'll be possible to lose a hectare or two of transgenic potatoes in their midst. Greg knows the farmer well. I'm sure he'll look after him.

Greg has always claimed not to be excited as I am. He plays this game with me: says he'd rather put a barrier up around this whole island. That organic is the way forward, and that if the public can see we're GM-free they'll *Buy British*. They'll buy from *Spudnik*. I'm not saying he's stupid, I love my brother.

'What's the wife reckon, then?' he provoked me yesterday, when I told him about AlphaGen and the trouble in Venezuela.

'You think I've told Lily?'

Greg gazed around the pub. Buying himself time to think things through. 'I wonder what Melody would say.'

'What the hell's Melody got to do with anything?' I said. 'Listen to what I'm telling you.'

'Technology is never inevitable,' Greg pointed out. 'The Aussies haven't built a single nuclear power station. They chose not to.'

'*This* technology can immunise, one day cure, people even while it feeds them,' I said. 'Look, you know full well genetic technology is different in kind. It's information. There are no barriers big enough to keep it out.'

Greg pretended he was unconvinced. It's his way of dealing with change. 'Tell me again how it's going to help us,' he demanded.

'Us? The company? This will be the biggest boost to the farming industry in a thousand years,' I told him. 'It's going to provide *Spudnik* with access to a new and lucrative market.'

He lifted his arms out wide in exasperation. 'I'm trying to cut out competition, and you're opening us up to it. Don't you think if you're on to this, the Dutch are, too?'

I laughed. 'Our competition's not going to come from Holland,' I said. 'The problem is that proteins become unstable in potatoes when they're cooked. And who wants to eat raw potato? No, the competition's going to come from tomatoes. From medical fruiterers reseeding the apple orchards of Kent. From hazel nuts in coppices in newly planted native woodland, programmed to grow at double speed. This is the future, brother. We've no time to waste.'

'If you're right. If everything's going to change,' Greg

said, 'there'll be endless public discussion. Committees. White papers. Green papers.'

'In due course,' I said. 'Of course. But we're talking about now. About who's in the lead. Don't go scared on me, now. The money's running right behind us.'

The very first potato growers were in the Andes. Modern-day Peru. High up on the altiplano. They were people who'd climbed out of the forest below, had fled from the terrors of the jungle. Impelled to grow out of their lives as savages, to escape being preyed upon by jaguar and boa constrictor, hemmed in by impenetrable undergrowth, by waters infested with alligator and voracious fish. Volatile tribes at shrieking war with one another, fighting with spear and poisoned arrow. A discordant life of oppressive tedium alternating with terror.

Or, if we prefer, they were people who'd been expelled from the innocent rainforest, where they dwelled with the spirits of their ancestors. Where they lived on a plentiful diet of fish and turtle, patches of manioc they cultivated in small clearings, and fruit they plucked from overabundant trees. A life of harmony. Take your pick.

These people – exiles or pioneers – climbed out of the lush montana, and sought places for settlement in the valleys of the high tablelands, where they domesticated llama and cultivated our *Solanum tuberosum*. And they survived the cold and the shortage of oxygen of that pitiless altitude, and its roaring driving rains.

This is progress. What can we do? We can't stop still. You stop still, you go round in circles. You go nowhere.

I dress our baby in the morning. His mother selects an outfit the night before and hangs it on the towel rail in the bathroom. There's a bewildering variety of design of the most basic items in a baby's wardrobe. During prenatal research into nappies, Lily bombarded me with outraged statistics about the amount of soiled disposables put into landfill sites each day, and waved brochures at me offering Terylene this, Velcro that. Snaps and poppers, cotton and cloth. Our boy is now secured with non-disposable unbleached cotton nappies, with a plastic outer wrap.

Then he wears a one-piece, a little leotard that fits down over his head and does up with three poppers at the crotch. Over this he wears a larger item, another all-in-one but with long arms and legs. Versions of this jumpsuit come in many different designs, though it has certain basic requirements i.e. fitting the baby and keeping him warm; being simple to open up and out of the way for nappy changing, and reasonably easy to change in and out of following inevitable spews and spills. There's one we have, from *Next*, I think, that meets these demands. It covers his torso and limbs in a comfortable balance between snug and loose; it's made of soft, thick cotton; you can slip it on and off; plus he looks good. These seem simple enough requirements, well met.

But some of the others people wouldn't believe. There's one with a home-boy hood and blue checks that's so tight and starchy it straitjackets him: sit John Junior up and he stays there, staring at you, stuck. There's another, a gift from an Italian friend of Lily's, that does up in so complicated a coming together of material at the back and sides that I have to flip the babe on to my lap and then on to his side, round and round, to painstakingly popper him up. And there's yet another that was designed for a baboon baby: it fits our boy's torso well enough but the arms and legs are twice as long as his and have to be folded back up, only they're very tight and can barely be persuaded to without cutting off the blood supply to his extremities.

'Why can't these people settle on one reasonable design and all use it?' I ranted at my wife yesterday morning, as I fumbled with ill-fitting buttons on a squirming baby (who I have to admit seemed unconcerned himself. John J. was fiddling with a label: he likes the satiny feel).

'I know,' Lily said. 'Let's all have Maoist babies, in identical little uniforms. I agree. But you could say the same about anything. Cars. Pens. Washing machines.'

'No,' I said. 'This is a very simple and singular case where the best design should clearly win out.'

'I'm not arguing,' she said. 'It's your system. Go on: you people defend it.'

I laughed. 'I can't,' I said. 'It stinks. Pass me that zinc and castor oil cream.'

This morning I lay in the spare bed, going over things in my mind, with my son asleep beside me. He stirred, hunger rumbling deep within him. Sometimes he wakes with ease, rising effortlessly into consciousness; opening his eyes, seeing me and smiling.

More often John Junior strains and fidgets in his sleep. It looks as if some unease is waking him, while at the same time a different unease is *thwarting* his attempt to wake himself. To struggle up out of this pit of sleep. Tossing his head from one side to another. Grimaces, baby groans.

Our son needs to wake and when he does I'll scoop him up before he becomes conscious of his empty stomach, and I'll carry him through to his sleeping mother. She'll wake even as we approach the bedroom, already be heaving herself up on to her elbows by the time we reach the bed; be groping for the feeding pillow, and the muslin with which she covers her spare, leaking breast. By then John Junior's hunger will be making itself known to him, but the sight of his mother will counteract this signal, and he'll smile at her as she sleepily greets him – 'Hello, gorgeous,' – as I pass him to her. His smile will engulf her nipple. He will guzzle milk from Lily's full breast.

This morning he needed to wake, but couldn't. He began to flail as if drowning in sleep. Our son could do with some help. I leaned over him and whispered, 'My darling, calm yourself. The day awaits, a life awaits you, this world is yours for the taking.' I kissed his forehead. 'Wake up, my beamish boy. Wake up.'

He is me. John Junior is my clone. Four hundred thousand pounds, he cost us. Worth every penny, I think. Ironic, isn't it? I couldn't reproduce, but I reproduced myself. If that's not creative, I don't know what is.

We want a girl next. It's Lily's turn, I suppose. A brother and a sister, like Mummy and Dad. Though me, I wouldn't mind another Melody. I think she deserves it. We'll see. We're just a bit short of cash right now. But I'm not worried. We've got Euro snacks. Crisper chips. We've got Edible Plant Vaccines. Something's coming up and we're going to make real money, and then we can do what we want.

## A NOTE ON THE AUTHOR

Tim Pears was born in 1956. He is the author of
three novels, *In the Place of Fallen Leaves* (winner
of the Hawthornden Prize for Literature and the
Ruth Hadden Award), *In a Land of Plenty* (which
was adapted into a major BBC TV Series in
2001) and *A Revolution of the Sun*. Tim Pears
lives in Oxford with his wife and two children.

## A NOTE ON THE TYPE

The text of this book is set in Linotype Sabon,
named after the type founder, Jacques Sabon.
It was designed by Jan Tschichold and jointly
developed by Linotype, Monotype and Stempel,
in response to a need for a typeface to be
available in identical form for mechanical hot
metal composition and hand composition using
foundry type.

Tschichold based his design for Sabon roman on a
fount engraved by Garamond, and Sabon italic on
a fount by Granjon. It was first used in 1966 and
has proved an enduring modern classic.